THE HUNTER HUNTED

THE HUNTER HUNTED

by

L. D. Tetlow

Dales Large Print Books
Long Preston, North Yorkshire,
England.

British Library Cataloguing in Publication Data.

Tetlow, L. D.
   The hunter hunted.

   A catalogue record for this book is
   available from the British Library

   ISBN 1-85389-765-5 pbk

First published in Great Britain by Robert Hale Ltd., 1996

Cover illustration © Lopez by arrangement with Allied Artists.

Published in Large Print 1997 by arrangement with Robert
Hale Ltd.

Dales Large Print is an imprint of
Library Magna Books Ltd.
Printed and bound in Great Britain by
T.J. International Ltd., Cornwall, PL28 8RW.

ONE

The silence, heavy and oppressive, filling the room with a chorus of as yet unasked and unanswered questions, questions to which there was no real answer, was nothing new to the large black man who stood alone in the centre of the saloon. His sardonic gaze slowly swept around the room, making a mental note of the occupants sitting at each table, the keen eyes missing nothing, not even the nervous twitch of a mouth. After taking in everything, the black man slowly ambled to the bar, where two men moved slowly to one side as if trying to avoid any possibility of physical contact. The black man smiled slightly and nodded to the bartender who was nervously cleaning a glass, a glass he had been cleaning ever since the black man walked into his saloon.

'Beer!' he growled.

The bartender slowly and carefully placed the now highly polished glass on to the counter and cast a nervous glance behind his seemingly unwelcome customer. 'He wants a beer!' he informed someone on the other side of the room.

The black man heard a chair scrape along the floor to be followed by slow, heavy, deliberate footsteps, but he did not look round. Instead he repeated his order for a beer.

'Bar's closed!' announced a deep voice from behind.

The black man smiled, nodded his head slightly and reached into his waistcoat pocket, an act which seemed to bring a flurry of nervous activity behind him. He slowly pulled out a large pocket watch, flicked the lid open and studied the face of the watch for a few moments before slowly replacing it in his waistcoat pocket and turning to face the man behind him. He showed no surprise when he saw the gun pointing at him nor at the man behind the gun and behind a sheriff's badge.

'Closed?' mused the black man. 'That's

just about the earliest I ever heard of a saloon closin'. Yes, sir, eight in the evenin' sure is early. Still, it is Sunday tomorrow an' I guess you all got to get back home to your beds so's you can be up nice an' early for church. Don't mind me, you just all go on home.'

'It's closed to the likes of you,' growled the sheriff. 'It's allus closed to the likes of you.'

'The likes of me?' grinned the black man. 'Who or what exactly is the likes of me? Perhaps you will allow me to introduce myself. Caleb Black, the Reverend Caleb Black, at your service. Yes, sir, Black by name an' black by birth. Tell me Sheriff, which of those two things about me is it that bothers you?'

The sheriff shuffled uneasily, nervously licking his lips while glancing from side to side. He slowly replaced his gun in its holster and then wiped his arm across his mouth. 'Reverend?' he queried. 'Sure, you're wearin' the clothes like I seen reverends wear but that don't mean nothin', you could be anyone just dressed to look like a minister.'

Once again, Caleb smiled and slowly reached into the inside pocket of his long, black coat and pulled out a folded paper which he offered to the sheriff. 'My certificate, issued by my church and recognized by those in power in Washington.'

The sheriff glared at Caleb but refused to take the paper. 'OK, so you're a minister, you got a piece of paper what proves it. There's just one thing that bothers me: you're just about the first reverend I ever seen wearin' a gun. Now I'm not an overly religious man, but I'd say a gun an' the pulpit don't sit too easily together.'

Caleb laughed. 'To you, perhaps not. Personally I have no difficulty in reconciling the two.' What Caleb chose not to tell the sheriff, for the moment at least, was that he earned the greater part of his income from bounty hunting. For the most part he picked up minor local outlaws with very small prices on their heads but occasionally he would also tackle the more infamous outlaws and thus earn himself several thousand dollars.

Sometimes he wondered why he bothered with the big-time outlaws since he invariably ended up giving the reward money away to a deserving cause. However, it pleased him to be able to look after local orphans and suchlike. His initial glance around the room had thrown up two faces he was quite certain appeared on some Wanted posters he was carrying, but he would check on that later. Right now his problem was with the sheriff and the obvious hostility of the other occupants of the saloon.

'We got certain laws in this town,' said the sheriff. 'Preacher or not, one of them laws is that no Blacks or Indians are allowed in the saloon. In fact it's against the law for Indians to drink hard liquor but I ain't too sure if that applies to Blacks or not.'

'I can assure you that it does not,' said Caleb. 'Nor is there any federal law which states that coloured people are not allowed in bars or saloons.'

11

'We got our own laws on things like that,' replied the sheriff, a little uncomfortable at being spoken to by a man who was obviously better educated than he and more especially since that man was also a Negro.

Caleb grinned broadly, spread his arms and shrugged. 'So much for the land where all men are free.'

'You're free,' grunted the sheriff. 'You're free to leave this town whenever you want.'

Caleb shook his head. 'I am not ready to leave just yet, Sheriff. I have travelled a long way and my horse is very tired and badly in need of rest, as am I. However, I am a man of peace and as such I shall not transgress your local laws even if they are less than fair, but I am very thirsty and would appreciate a large glass of beer. Is there any law against someone bringing it out to me on the sidewalk?'

The sheriff was plainly completely baffled, he had never had a Black or an Indian dare to answer him back before. He looked about the saloon hoping that someone would give him some guidance but it appeared that almost everyone was in the same position he was. There were a few muffled voices suggesting that the preacher be thrown out there and then but most remained silent. Eventually the sheriff sighed and nodded to the bartender.

'Give him a beer to take outside,' he said. He looked hard at Caleb. 'That's all, just the one.'

'I thank you for your kindness,' grinned Caleb, leaving the sheriff with the distinct impression that he had just been slighted, but he could not really be certain.

The beer was handed to Caleb, who in turn handed over a silver dollar and waited for his change, which did not appear to be forthcoming. Eventually, at a grunt from the sheriff, some coins were handed back to Caleb who did not bother to count them. He was quite certain that he had been overcharged but he felt that he had at least established certain ground-rules between himself and the residents of West Ridge.

Caleb had been travelling for more than a week, during which time he had encountered only one sign of humanity and civilization—a remote homestead occupied by a very poor white family. Desperately poor they might have been, but they had willingly shared what food they had and had seemed overwhelmed when Caleb had offered to make their relationship legal by performing a marriage ceremony. The woman had told him that they had never undergone any form of marriage and had brought four children into the world during the past six years. She appeared to be more pleased for her children than for herself, saying that at least they would now be legitimate. Caleb was not too certain as to the actual legality of such a thing, but he knew that it really did not matter.

West Ridge, according to the battered sign about a mile out of town, boasted a population of just over 500. He also discovered that part of the town he first came to supported one saloon, a shabby looking hotel, a bank, a general store and a hardware store and, plainly the mainstay

14

of the local economy and seemingly the sole employer, a timber yard and sawmill. It was difficult to see where the products of the sawmill were sold, but it gave the impression of being quite busy. He later found that timber was transported to a railroad some twenty miles away. He also discovered that the hardware store doubled as a barber and bath-house and was a little surprised that he was allowed to partake of its services.

Outside the saloon it appeared that word had spread rapidly about a Negro who had demanded and had been given a drink in the saloon, even outside. The very fact of a black man handling a glass of beer was a first in West Ridge. It seemed that almost everyone in town and beyond had come to look at this unusual stranger and Caleb could not resist growling at one small boy who had stood staring at him for about ten minutes. The resultant scream from the child brought a tirade of abuse from a man who was apparently his father. Despite this, the effect was that the curious quickly realized that they had other things to do and everyone slowly dispersed, all except a group of five middle-aged women who talked in whispers amongst themselves whilst constantly casting nervous glances at Caleb. His response was to smile at the ladies and raise his hat to them.

After about ten minutes of whispering and glancing, the oldest looking of the women coughed self-consciously and falteringly approached him.

'Excuse me, sir,' she said, obviously in some discomfort at having to address him as '*sir*'. 'Is it true that you are an ordained preacher?' Caleb gave her a broad smile and nodded. 'I...I...I mean a real preacher, you know, a preacher from the recognized church?'

'That I am, ma'am,' grinned Caleb. 'The Reverend Caleb Black, at your service.' He pulled the piece of paper he had offered the sheriff out of his pocket and handed it to the woman. 'As you can see, it proves that I am indeed an ordained minister, fully qualified to carry out baptisms, marriages and funerals and to administer the sacraments.'

16

She glanced nervously at the paper, smiled thinly and handed it back to him. 'I'm sorry if I seemed to doubt you,' she said. 'It's just that we have never seen a...' She looked at her companions nervously.

Caleb laughed. 'I'm used to it, ma'am,' he said reassuringly. 'That's the reason I carry that certificate. Everyone seems to accept it when a white man claims to be a priest or a minister but they always have doubts about a Negro. That goes for my own kind as well, they don't seem to believe it either. Yes, ma'am, I am what I claim to be. What can I do for you?'

The woman was now joined by her companions and they seemed a little more relaxed but they seemed reluctant to join him on the boardwalk outside the saloon. He had met these women many times in various parts of the country; even the idea of being seen standing outside a den of iniquity such as a saloon filled them with horror and shame. He decided to save them further embarrassment by joining them in the street and walking a few yards away from the saloon where he

17

repeated his question.

The eldest woman spoke, as seemed only natural, she was apparently the leader of the group. 'Reverend,' she said quietly as if trying to disguise the fact that she was even talking to him, 'you probably saw the church as you came into town...' In actual fact Caleb had not seen any sign of a church but he simply nodded. 'Not a very pretty building I must admit,' she continued. 'The last time it was used for the purpose it was built, was three years ago. In those days we had a preacher living in the town but he suddenly died and we were never sent a replacement even though we have requested one many times...'

'And you want me to conduct a service?' smiled Caleb.

The women looked nervously at each other and nodded sagely. 'Of course we don't expect you to become permanent,' blushed one of the other ladies, 'but we know that a great many townsfolk and a few from the outlying homesteads would be only too grateful to attend a proper service again.'

'Your menfolk didn't seem too pleased to see me,' reminded Caleb. 'They certainly didn't want me in their bar. Perhaps they thought that being black I wouldn't be so noticeable out here in the dark.'

The ladies shuffled a little uneasily and Caleb sensed that if the truth were to be told, they too would rather not have a coloured man in town, preacher or not. They all assured him that their men were not really like that and in any case *their* husbands certainly did not frequent such places—not very often that was. However, it was plain that his services as a minister were needed to the extent that they were prepared to accept the sacraments from almost anyone.

Caleb smiled, accepting the situation for what it was and nodded reassuringly. 'It will be my pleasure, ladies,' he said. 'Unless my travels through the deserts and plains this past few weeks have made me become a little forgetful, by my calculation it is Sunday tomorrow. That being the case, are you quite certain that you can organize things by then?'

'Quite certain,' assured the leader of the ladies. 'The preacher we had before usually held his morning service at about ten o'clock. Would such a time be agreeable to you?'

'Perfect!' grinned Caleb. 'Mind you, if the church has not been used for three years I dare say it will require some work and organizing.'

'The church will be ready!' asserted one of the other ladies. 'We thank you, Reverend. Now, we really must be getting along, it is most unseemly for a lady to be seen on the streets at this time of night.'

Caleb smiled again and raised his hat as they nodded at him and wandered off along the street but it was noticeable that they did not walk too quickly and giggled amongst themselves when they received a couple of whistles from lone men.

The next problem which faced Caleb was the question of accommodation. Since the town had laws about who could and could not drink in its saloons, he would not have been at all surprised if the only hotel also applied the same rule. It was not that he minded sleeping anywhere, indeed during his life he had slept in some very strange places, but at that moment he felt that he had the upper hand in the town and resolved to push it as far as he could.

As expected, the little man whom Caleb took to be the clerk but proved to be the owner, one Silas Green, at first appeared to be very reluctant to accept Caleb as a paying guest. His first excuse was that the hotel was full, but when Caleb turned the register to examine who was booked in, he found that the hotel was in fact completely empty.

'Your sign says three dollars a night, includin' evenin' meal and breakfast,' grinned Caleb. 'That seems fair to me.'

'Er...all the bedclothes are in the wash,' protested Silas.

'That's OK,' smiled Caleb, 'just give me the room. I've slept in my underclothes so long now that it won't matter for another night. I'll expect a fifty cent reduction in the price of course.'

Silas seemed to have no further excuses

to offer except one. 'It's the wife; she'd kill me if I let you in. For myself it don't matter who the hell you are, you understand, but women are peculiar creatures and they don't come any more peculiar than my wife.'

At that moment one of the ladies who had met Caleb outside the saloon burst in and suddenly stopped and looked at the preacher with a slightly horrified expression, which she quickly tried to hide.

'He's lookin' for a room,' explained Silas. 'I've already told him that...'

'Of course!' gushed Mrs Green with obvious embarrassment. 'I should have thought about it myself, it's just that I was too tied up with the Townswomens' Committee.' She turned and scowled at her husband, trying to hide her face from Caleb. 'Silas, the best room in the house for the reverend.'

Silas was completely taken aback by the sudden turn of events and the insistence of his wife that a black man be allowed over the hallowed steps of the hotel. He shook his head but chose not to question the sudden change in the house rules and took a key off a board behind him and handed it to Caleb. 'First floor, opposite the stairs, at the front,' he said.

'Silas!' exclaimed Mrs Green—Caleb never did discover what her given name was and it never seemed appropriate to ask. 'You can't expect the reverend to carry his bags up to his room...' She looked about for Caleb's luggage. 'Oh, oh I see you do not appear to have any baggage with you...'

Caleb smiled. 'Only what's on my horse. That's OK, I've got to stable her anyhow, I'll bring it up. Now, your sign says somethin' about evenin' meal, ma'am. I am kind of hungry.'

'Evening meal!' The prospect seemed to fill Mrs Green with considerable alarm, so much so that she scuttled off into the rear of the building, shouting some muffled instructions at her husband as she went. Silas simply smiled at Caleb in wonderment.

'Mister,' he grinned, 'reverend or no reverend, I ain't never seen her like this before. Even the last minister we had here was as much afraid of her as anyone else, an' believe me that's everyone in town 'ceptin' Mrs Stein. Nobody argues with Mrs Stein, not even my wife. No sir, I don't know what it is you got on her but she sure seems afraid of you.'

'Maybe it's this!' grinned Caleb, stroking his face.

Silas looked puzzled at first, but as Caleb again stroked his face a broad grin spread across Silas's face. 'Hell, now that's a turn up. Yeh, you're a preacher, but you're a black preacher.' He laughed loudly and suddenly clamped his hand across his mouth and stared in mock horror at Caleb. He eventually released his hand.

'Yeh, a preacher she can deal with an' a Negro she can deal with, but when the two are the same, she just don't know how to cope.' He became a little more serious. 'Mind you, she's a fast learner so I wouldn't count on things bein' so good for much longer.' A sudden loud shout from the bowels of the hotel made him laugh again but he was quick to obey the call.

Caleb did not bother to take a look at his room, instead he returned to where he had left his horse, outside the saloon and, apart from two swaggering youths who deliberately did not see him but who felt the force of his body as he too quite deliberately walked between them and then turned and apologized for not seeing them, the interest in him seemed to have evaporated. The youths were not quite sure what to do, but the sight of a gun on the preacher's upper thigh had the effect of making their actions quite determined—they ran!

The fact that Caleb wore a gun had been noted and remarked upon by all the men in the saloon earlier and the sheriff had commented on it to Caleb. What none of them had seen however, was that this particular gun-toting preacher was also a two-gun man. Normally both guns were covered by Caleb's long coat, but he was not averse to letting anyone see that he wore one gun but he rarely showed two.

In the past the wearing of two guns had proved Caleb's saviour as everyone had assumed that he had only one and when, on occasion, he had been disarmed—or so it was thought—his other gun had saved his life.

At the far end of town, previously unseen by Caleb, he found a livery stable, two more stores—a drapery store which displayed the name of 'Stein' and an undertaker and carpentry store—and the sheriff's office and jail.

The blacksmith, who owned the livery stable, accepted Caleb's horse without question and without saying a word, despite Caleb's questioning. It was only later that he discovered that the blacksmith, Patrick O'Hara, was also deaf and dumb.

As he left the livery stable, the sheriff was waiting for him on the steps of his office and called him over. 'I hear the ladies have asked you to take a service,' he remarked.

'Correct,' said Caleb. 'It would appear that even a black preacher has his uses.'

'Guess so,' admitted the sheriff. 'I'm still

puzzled about you though, colour of your skin apart, it ain't usual for a preacher to carry a gun, especially a preacher who looks like he knows how to use it and ain't afraid to either.'

Caleb mounted the step and stood alongside the sheriff, towering a good foot over him. He looked down and smiled, knowing that this action alone was intimidating. 'Army training,' explained Caleb. 'I had me three years in the army before becoming a man of the cloth.'

The sheriff looked up at him and shook his head. 'Naw, that ain't it. Sure, you've got a military bearing, but that ain't it. No, I'd say you know how to use a gun in the way a gunfighter knows, not the way you was taught in the army I was in the army too once, long time ago. Sergeant I was. I don't suppose you ever made sergeant.'

'Lieutenant!' said Caleb.

'Lieutenant?' said the sheriff looking up sharply. 'How come?'

'Special black unit,' explained Caleb The sheriff thought for a moment and then nodded. 'Yeh, I seem to remember hearin' about that. Lieutenant eh! Seems to me the whole world's turned upside down.'

'It seems to me that some lawmen don't appear to know or care about wanted outlaws either,' said Caleb.

The sheriff's eyes glared up at Caleb for a moment, showing an underlying mistrust and even hatred. 'What the hell do you mean by that?' he demanded.

'Just that there's at least two men in town, or were in town when I was in the saloon, who have rewards out on them.'

'Oh, yeh!' grated the sheriff. 'Just who?'

Caleb pulled a wad of Wanted posters from the bag he was carrying and, holding them in the light from the sheriff's office, thumbed through them for a while, eventually pulling two out and showing them to the sheriff who only gave them a cursory glance before handing them back to Caleb.

'I note that you seem to know them,' observed Caleb.

'Ain't never seen 'em in my life!'

'Pete Coyne and Al Gates,' read Caleb.

'Yes, it was them. I saw them in the saloon. One thing I never do is forget a face. They're not worth that much, I grant you, but even seventy five dollars each is not to be overlooked too lightly.'

'You're the first stranger through West Ridge in four weeks,' said the sheriff. 'If they'd been here I'd've known. Anyhow, them drawings could be almost anyone.'

'Not in this case,' assured Caleb. 'The scar across Gates's forehead was very plain to see.'

The sheriff shuffled a little uneasily before looking up at Caleb again. 'What if they were here?' he said. 'What's it to you? You're in the business of savin' people's souls.'

'Part of the time,' admitted Caleb, 'but that does not provide me with a steady income. For a good many years I have had to supplement my earnings by bounty hunting.'

TWO

Caleb had spent a somewhat restless night, nothing to do with the bed, which was as comfortable as any he had slept in, more to do with the fact that he had somehow anticipated trouble. He had immediately regretted admitting to the sheriff that in addition to being a preacher, he was also a bounty hunter.

The men he had seen in the saloon were the outlaws Coyne and Gates, he was quite certain of that just as he quite certain that the two were still in West Ridge. He was just as certain that, despite the sheriff's denial, he knew all about them and had more than likely rushed to tell them what Caleb had said almost as soon as he could.

However, his concerns had proved unfounded, at least for the moment although it had happened in the past that such men had sought to eliminate him whilst he was asleep. Although he had thought that he had spent most of the night listening for the telltale creak of floorboards and the muffled whisper, he must have slept more than he had imagined since he was not as tired as he might have expected.

At breakfast it appeared that he was, in fact, the only resident of the hotel, which came as no surprise. Breakfast consisted of a large ham, two eggs, an unidentifiable mess of something fried which actually tasted quite good, followed by two mugs of coffee. Mrs Green busy-bodied around him as if frightened he might suddenly disappear or change his mind about taking service that morning, all the time assuring him that even as he ate, the ladies of the town were making the church fit for human habitation.

The appointed hour came and Caleb once again found himself being fussed over, this time with the overbearing Mrs Stein appearing to take control. The two women, Mrs Stein and Mrs Green, placed themselves either side of their preacher as if escorting a prisoner—which in many ways was exactly what Caleb felt like—and proudly and almost defiantly, marched him to the church.

The reason Caleb had not noticed the building as he rode into town—apart from the fact that it had been dark—was that it was situated off the main street behind a clump of trees. A long, low building with only a solitary bell which was at that moment pealing out its monotonous chime, there was no other indication that this was or had been a church. The cemetery, he later discovered, was situated some distance up the hill behind the building.

Actually, Caleb was very surprised at the size of the congregation and he was forced to wonder if this was due to faith or could be more accurately attributed to curiosity—curiosity as to how a black preacher would perform. He had little doubt that many of the men had been forced into their Sunday clothes by their womenfolk and ordered to be on their best behaviour. Various small children, too young to appreciate the curiosity value of the preacher, played in and out between the adults but the older boys looked almost resentful at being forced into clothes they were completely unaccustomed to and glared at Caleb as if it were all his fault.

Most of the girls used the opportunity to flaunt themselves and their finery before the best of West Ridge's young manhood and indulge in a lot of flirtation. The older women of the town had, it seemed, also taken the opportunity to use the occasion to show off the extent and finery of their wardrobes as well as apparently trying to prove that they could each produce the best-dressed husband in town.

The service seemed to meet with universal approval, even Caleb's sermon which he had deliberately based on brotherly love and acceptance no matter what the colour of a man's skin. Afterwards there was hardly a person who would admit to having any form of bias because of race, although those same people also claimed that it was fear of pressure from less understanding neighbours which shaped their attitudes.

Actually Caleb found the complete honesty of one family, seemingly quite important in the community, quite refreshing when they almost proudly admitted that they were originally from a slave-owning family and greatly regretted the passing of the slave-owning days, saying that slavery was the preordained lot of almost all coloured people. However, they did treat Caleb with respect and not the falseness that oozed from almost everyone else.

As they all gathered in front of the church afterwards, Mrs Stein, with Mrs Green proudly at her side, took it upon herself to make a speech thanking their unexpected visitor for performing a much needed function and even suggesting that he, Caleb, would be welcome to remain in the town—at least until a permanent replacement was delivered to them.

Suddenly Caleb found himself under siege from various mothers bearing young children with requests for christenings and by five couples, three of whom also bore young children, for weddings. Caleb was becoming quite concerned by the turn of events; it had certainly not been his intention to remain in West Ridge and it still was not his intention, but there was quite plainly a need for a minister although he knew that that minister was not going to be him. However, he felt that he must at least fulfil the immediate need and agreed to perform all the necessary functions requested during the forthcoming week, stressing that when he had finished, he would be on his way.

The collection plate proved another surprise, providing him with eighty-four dollars and fifty-two cents, two buttons and three Mexican coins. The eighty-four dollars gave him much needed funds which, with the charges he would make for the performance of christenings and marriages, would mean that he would probably be about one hundred dollars the richer when he eventually departed West Ridge. In addition to this, Mrs Green informed him that he was quite welcome to stay at the hotel free of charge—apart from the cost of food. He suspected that she had been forced into that position by Mrs Stein.

Even the sheriff had turned up in his best clothes and had congratulated Caleb on his performance as if he had been witness to some circus act. He made no reference to Caleb's revelation about being a bounty hunter, but it had been very noticeable that neither of the outlaws was to be seen, a fact Caleb put down to their having been warned.

'Don't you ever take that gun off?' asked the sheriff as the crowd began to disperse. Once again he had assumed that Caleb only wore one gun.

'Not very often,' Caleb admitted. 'I even had to use it in church once, when some outlaws decided the congregation were easy pickings.'

'What happened to them?'

'Well they might have been killed in a house of God but I don't suppose that gave them automatic entry to Heaven.'

'You killed 'em!' exclaimed the sheriff. 'In a church as well! That sure don't fit with no preacher I ever met before.'

Caleb laughed. 'We're all only human, you know; we come in all shapes and sizes just like real people and we even have the same ideas and feelings of real people.'

'But most real people don't go round huntin' outlaws,' observed the sheriff. 'Leastways not most people I know.'

'True!' grinned Caleb. 'But I don't exactly go hunting outlaws, I usually only take the ones who happen to drop into my lap so to speak.'

'Like the two you saw yesterday?' asked the sheriff.

'Like the two I saw yesterday,' agreed Caleb. 'It's my guess I missed my chance there.'

The sheriff looked slightly uncomfortable and said nothing, deciding that he needed to talk to someone else and left Caleb to the mercy of Mrs Stein and Mrs Green who were rapidly bearing down on them.

'Lovely sermon, Reverend,' gushed Mrs Stein. 'So true, it's such a pity that more can't live in peace together. I hope the message was not lost on certain members of our community.'

Caleb smiled to himself. From what he had seen of Mrs Stein, he would have great difficulty in living at peace with her. Her intentions might have been very good but it was plain that her version of living in peace was for her and her ladies committee to take over everything, especially her.

The small talk continued for a few more minutes and ended with Caleb being offered what Mrs Stein insisted was correctly called 'lunch' at her house. As much as he would have liked to, Caleb could not think of any feasible excuse as to why he should refuse. He even cast a surreptitious glance towards the heavens in a silent prayer that there might be some divine intervention.

He gained brief respite by insisting that he must return to his room and clean himself up, raised his hat and quickly departed before either Mrs Stein or Mrs Green could say anything else. As he left, Mrs Stein called out that lunch would be on the table at one o'clock sharp. This information had the distinct overtones of various drill sergeants he had known during his army service and one did not argue with drill sergeants.

The time between going back to his room at the hotel and the time to go to lunch with Mrs Stein seemed to pass with twice the speed of normal time and he looked at his watch more than once convinced that it must have gone wrong, but he knew that it was functioning perfectly. He finally sighed heavily, looked at himself in a long mirror, at the guns he was wearing and reluctantly decided that a lunch with Mrs Stein was hardly the place to display his hardware.

Downstairs he was surprised to meet Silas Green, still dressed in his best clothes and looking most uncomfortable in a high, starched collar. Silas did in fact appear to be waiting for him.

'I've been instructed to escort the condemned man,' Silas grinned weakly. 'Me an' the wife have been invited as well.'

'Now I know just how a man must feel as he's led to the gallows,' smiled Caleb. 'I suppose I shouldn't be uncharitable, it must have caused Mrs Stein some considerable anguish to offer a Negro a place at her table, be he a preacher or not.'

Silas laughed. 'Oh, don't you worry none about that, Reverend, she'll make capital out of this episode for years to come. She'll make it plain to everyone what a sacrifice she made. That woman never does nothin' but that she gains somethin' out of it.'

'It's hard to see what,' said Caleb.

'She'll think of somethin', if she ain't already done so,' grinned Silas.

The two men stepped outside, the diminutive Silas and the towering Caleb, a very odd couple and the incongruity of it was not lost on various others in the street, although none laughed out loud.

They had hardly stepped off the board-walk to cross the street when Caleb suddenly grabbed Silas's arm and pulled him up. 'My guns, I forgot my guns!'

'What you want your guns for?' asked Silas quite alarmed. 'Folk round here don't wear guns, 'specially on Sunday. Most folk, me included, hardly know how to handle one. I know the prospect of eatin' with Mrs Stein is almost life threatenin', but I don't think you'll need a gun to deal with her.'

The reasons for Caleb suddenly deciding that he needed his guns were standing outside the saloon across the street and he nodded briefly at them, although it appeared that neither man had seen him. He turned and ran back to his room where he quickly fastened his two belts, checked each gun and adjusted the lie of his long coat briefly. A quick glance out of the window across the street showed that Coyne and Gates had disappeared.

Caleb now found himself in a somewhat difficult position. His first impulse was to go after the two men and collect the reward but common sense told him that this was not the time. The chances were that they would be around for some time yet. He toyed with the idea of removing his guns again but finally decided, risking the disapproval of Mrs Stein, that keeping them on was the logical thing to do. At lunch he would hang them up along with his coat and hope that he did not have to justify himself to the ladies.

Outside, Silas looked Caleb up and down and grinned slightly. 'I reckon I must be just about the only man in this town who knows you wear two guns,' he said. 'I seen that when you checked in. You make it plain you wear one but keep the other well covered. Can you use both?'

'I wouldn't waste my time wearing them if I couldn't,' said Caleb. 'Where did those two men go?'

'Inside the saloon,' replied Silas. 'Why are you so worried about them?'

'Outlaws,' said Caleb.

'You know them?'

'Not personally,' admitted Caleb, 'but I know who they are and, more importantly, I reckon they know just who I am as well by now.'

'Everyone in town knows who you are,' said Silas, 'an' most of 'em ain't too keen on seein' black skins about the place, but that don't mean anyone's out to kill you.'

'Let's hope not,' sighed Silas, 'not yet awhile at least. OK, let's get over to Mrs Stein. One o'clock she said and I reckon that's just what she meant, not one minute past.'

Silas smiled and nodded in agreement and they crossed the street, walking along the boardwalk past the saloon, where Caleb half expected the two men to come out of the door in front of them. His expectations were not far out, the swing doors crashed open just after they had passed.

'Hold it right there Mr Preacherman!' came the rasping order. Both Caleb and Silas held it where they were, Caleb with his hand poised ready to move. 'Turn round, real slow,' came another command. Once again both Caleb and Silas obeyed.

'We ain't got the time to talk,' said Silas, choking back a lump in his throat. 'We're havin' dinner with Mrs Stein an' we're late already an' Mrs Stein ain't one to be kept waitin'.'

The two men laughed and Coyne waved his gun. 'This ain't nothin' to do with you, little man; on your way, don't keep Mrs

Stein waitin'. It's the preacher here we got business with.'

Silas glanced at Caleb, smiled weakly and suddenly leapt off the boardwalk, running in the direction of the Stein house and the sheriff's office. If he was going for the sheriff, Caleb somehow knew that he would not be easy to find.

'What's your business?' asked Caleb, quietly.

'I reckon you know exactly,' snarled Gates. 'We hear tell that you is a bounty hunter an' that you got your eyes set on the reward out on us. We don't like bounty hunters. Most of all we don't like black bounty hunters.'

'So what are you going to do about it?' asked Caleb, deliberately trying to goad the men.

'Kill you,' replied Coyne in a matter-of-fact way. 'We could've just shot you in the back, it sure would have been easier, but we just thought that at least you ought to know what you're dyin' for.'

'Then kill me!' invited Caleb, flicking back the other side of his coat to reveal his other gun. For a moment both men looked alarmed and shuffled slightly.

'Two guns!' grunted Gates. 'It ain't often you see a man wearin' two guns. Thing is, two guns or not, there's two pointed straight at you.'

'Now that would be a stupid move,' Caleb pointed out. 'Shooting me in cold blood would be murder and as far as I know neither of you is wanted for murder just yet. Murder would up the price on your heads an' make you all the more rewardin' for other bounty hunters.'

'Can you use them guns?' sneered Coyne.

'Try me!' invited Caleb.

The two men shuffled a little uneasily, licked their lips and glanced at each other. That glance may have been brief but it was sufficient for Caleb to act which, despite his size, he could do very quickly.

Three shots rang out, echoing off the buildings and two men fell to the boardwalk. The third shot splintered the wood alongside Caleb's ear.

The street was suddenly alive with

people, people who had previously quickly discovered other things to do at the first sign of trouble and they now all stared in awe at this strange preacher. More significantly the sheriff also appeared, pushing through the swing doors of the saloon, calling for everyone to keep calm but since there was no panic at all, his instructions seemed entirely inappropriate, however, it appeared to do something for his ego as he kept repeating the instruction.

Caleb, in the meantime, had knelt down to examine the bodies and quickly confirmed that both men were dead. He looked up at the sheriff and smiled thinly, almost sneeringly. 'So where were you when the action started?' he asked.

'I was out the back, in the privy,' grunted the sheriff.

'Very fortunate,' sneered Caleb, 'I suppose you thought all you'd have to do was come out an' pick the pieces; namely me?'

'I didn't know nothin' about what they intended doin',' objected the sheriff. 'I didn't even know they was back in town.'

'Fair fight, Sheriff!' assured a man standing nearby. 'I seen it all, they came out lookin' for trouble, all the Reverend did was protect himself, I heard one of 'em say he was goin' to kill him.'

'I ain't questionin' if it was a fair fight or not,' glowered the sheriff, 'I'll take the Reverend's word for it. Right now I want these bodies movin'.'

'I reckon Jake'll be along with his wagon any moment now,' laughed another man. 'I just seen him harin' back to his place an' he don't run unless he's got the scent of a few dollars' business.'

Jake Bannon, the undertaker, proved this statement correct by suddenly arriving with his hearse. There were no formalities or reverence, the bodies were roughly handled into the hearse and it was driven rapidly away, leaving the centre of West Ridge as though nothing had ever happened. Caleb smiled, the scene was not new. Violent death, although something of a rarity even in places like West Ridge and especially if it concerned strangers, was a passing moment, the victims given little thought almost as soon as their bodies were taken away.

Caleb looked at the sheriff and smiled again. 'I reckon I just earned myself another hundred and fifty dollars, seventy five each at the last count.'

'I reckon you just earned yourself a one-way ticket to wherever it is you're destined for,' grunted the sheriff.

'Meaning what, precisely?' asked Caleb.

The sheriff looked at Caleb and sighed heavily. 'Maybe you'd better come to my office an' I'll explain,' he said.

'You can do your explaining later!' came the sharp retort. Both men turned to see Mrs Stein mounting the step. 'I've got a good meal laid out for you, Reverend,' she scolded, 'too good to waste. Now I don't know what happened here other than Silas saying something about two men wanting to kill you and I don't much care.'

Caleb smiled and raised his hat. 'It wasn't much,' he said to her, 'just a

48

little difference of opinion. I'm coming right along.' He turned to the sheriff. 'I'll be in your office at four, we do have some things to sort out.'

THREE

Caleb had expected Mrs Stein to be somehow shocked at the thought of a minister of the church wearing guns and even more shocked at that same minister killing people, be they outlaws or not. In fact, Mrs Stein insisted on hearing all the gory details. If anyone was shocked, it was Mrs Green, but she could not show her horror purely because Mrs Stein did not show any. It simply was not done for anyone to express a different view or reaction to Mrs Stein.

Caleb decided to use the moment to explain to the ladies that he was no ordinary preacher, expecting Mrs Stein to refuse to have anything to do with him again, which would have suited him. However, his admittance to being a bounty hunter seemed to fire Mrs Stein's imagination and she insisted on listening to some of his exploits.

There was no Mr Stein, he had departed West Ridge some five years previously and Caleb was not quite certain if that meant that he had died or that he had simply departed West Ridge. His natural feeling was for the latter.

Mr Stein, or to give him his correct title Major Stein, had served with the Corps of Engineers for most of his life, eventually being forced out through medical disability but, although he had had some dealings with the engineers, the name of Stein meant nothing to Caleb.

Eventually Mrs Stein gave clear indication that what was in effect an audience was at an end. She did not exactly say that it was ended, but her manner left little room for doubt.

It was almost four o'clock and Caleb took his leave of the regal Mrs Stein and went across the street to the sheriff's office, noticing for the first time a painted sign which proclaimed the sheriff's name, Matthew Brent. The sheriff was sitting at his desk thumbing through a sheaf of papers which he placed to one side as the preacher entered.

'I see you finally escaped the clutches of our Mrs Stein,' he smiled. 'A truly formidable woman in many ways, but she does have the interests of West Ridge close to her heart.'

'A fine woman,' said Caleb, 'if a little overpowering.'

'That's what her husband thought,' smiled Brent. 'She likes to give everyone the impression that she's a widow, but the truth is he walked out on her.'

Caleb smiled as he seated himself opposite the sheriff, somehow pleased that his impression had been proved correct. 'Now, Sheriff, you said you had something to explain. Well, I'm here and I'm all ears.'

Matt Brent looked a little uneasy and pulled the sheaf of papers closer to him. 'I know you didn't have much alternative but to shoot those men, but it may well prove to be most unfortunate both for you and for the town of West Ridge...'

'How can it be unfortunate to rid any

town of known outlaws?' asked Caleb.

Brent pulled the top piece of paper off the pile and handed it to Caleb, saying nothing but indicating that he should read it. There was silence for a few moments as Caleb digested the information and then handed it back to the sheriff.

'OK, so I've read it. How does Gill Weston fit in even if he does have quite a record for violence and murder? The only thing about him that would interest me is the three thousand dollar reward.'

'That's exactly what a few others thought too,' said Brent. 'So far we've buried five would-be bounty hunters. Gill Weston is the leader of a gang of outlaws who have more or less taken up permanent residence somewhere in the forest. They've been there for almost two years now and have set themselves up in a nice little business of extorting money from the logging company. In effect they levy a charge on every tree that's felled.'

Caleb nodded, realizing the implication of what he had done. 'And I take it Coyne and Gates were members of that gang.'

'Right first time,' sighed Brent. 'They were Weston's eyes and ears in town, they kept a check on exactly what the logging company was doing, regularly counting the trees which were brought in and acting as collectors for the money.'

'Why didn't you arrest them? You knew they were wanted men.'

'I don't know how many men Weston has out there,' said Brent, 'but it's at least ten, not includin' Coyne and Gates. Weston made it quite clear that if anything was to happen to either of them there would be reprisals on West Ridge. Exactly what those reprisals would be was never made clear, but the town council and the logging company decided that it was not worth taking the chance of anyone getting killed.'

'What levy does he put on the trees?'

'Two dollars a tree, no matter the size,' said Brent. 'The company can stand that, they get a good price for timber.'

Caleb smiled sardonically. 'So ten men, twelve at the most, can hold a town with a population of something over five hundred to ransom. Purely from a logistical point of view, I'd say that the odds were very much against this Gill Weston.'

The sheriff looked a little sheepish and coughed nervously. 'So would I,' he admitted. 'Only thing is out of about five hundred in town, roughly half are women, a quarter children under the age of sixteen and of the rest, about half are old men over sixty. In addition there's some thirty loggers at the camp out in the forest.'

'Still more than enough,' said Caleb.

Brent sighed heavily. 'I don't know where you come from, Reverend, or where you've been, but West Ridge has always been a peaceful town. The folk here just don't know how to handle situations like this. You wear two guns and it seems you know how to use them. Apart from me, I doubt if there's more than four other men who are capable of handling guns, even if they had them. I've got a rack over there with ten rifles, all of them so old they're probably more danger to the man who fires them than who they are aimed at. Apart

55

from mine I doubt if there's one modern weapon in town. What few guns there are are only shotguns.'

Caleb thought for a moment. He could appreciate the problem that West Ridge was faced with and providing the logging company were prepared to pay the levy of two dollars he could see why anyone was reluctant to tackle outlaws who would kill without thinking. From what he had heard and seen he doubted if any man, with the possible exception of the sheriff, would have the nerve to actually pull the trigger and end another man's life.

He was somewhat surprised that Mrs Stein had not told him of the situation, especially with her undoubted interest for the more gory details of his escapades and he could only put it down to her reluctance to become in any way more beholden to a man of his colour than she already was. Pride, it seemed, was Mrs Stein's Achilles' heel.

Caleb and the sheriff talked for some time and Caleb's first impression of mistrust rapidly gave way to one of understanding as to why the sheriff had acted the way he had. He had no doubts that news of the deaths of Coyne and Gates had even now reached the ears of Gill Weston and he could imagine the town bracing itself for the expected reprisal.

Sheriff Brent made no objection to paying the reward money to the preacher, except that he would have to wait until the bank opened in the morning, although he did express the opinion that it would be a waste of time since he, Caleb, would more than likely be dead before he could spend any of it.

There had been one other question which had been troubling Caleb, even if only slightly, and that was exactly why the town was so much against Negroes. The explanation was that when the logging company had first moved in some ten years previously, they had brought with them a large labour force, almost entirely black, and these men had caused so much trouble and ill-feeling that the company had been forced to dismiss them. Some had lingered in the town for a short while but eventually they had all left. Ever since then there had been a strong feeling against Negroes.

Caleb accepted this explanation but could not but question what feelings would have been had those men been white and still caused the same amount of trouble. The sheriff had no answer to that.

Walking back along the street to his hotel the effect of the killings and the realization of what they entailed was quite plain to Caleb. Without exception, everyone avoided him in some way, either by crossing the street or by suddenly disappearing into doorways or down side alleys. At the hotel even Silas and Mrs Green seemed reluctant to talk to him and he would not have been surprised to have been told that his room was no longer vacant, but things had not gone quite that far. However, Silas Green silently and solemnly handed Caleb two notes, both from people who had requested the baptisms of their children stating that they had now changed their minds.

During the evening other notes arrived all cancelling various arrangements made earlier that day. It was quite plain that the town of West Ridge was rapidly seeking to disassociate itself from the man who had killed the outlaws. As to whether this would do any good or not, Caleb had serious doubts, but his sympathy was with the townsfolk and he could well appreciate their actions.

The mood being as it was, Caleb decided not to aggravate things any further by going to the saloon, as had been his intention. His evening meal was provided in sullen silence and he returned to his room where he pondered his situation. Eventually he accepted the inevitable and decided that he would leave West Ridge in the morning. He even considered leaving before the bank opened and collecting his money, but the defiant streak in him decided that since the money was legally his, he would take it.

There followed another uneasy night, although he doubted if Gill Weston would act before daylight.

At breakfast the following morning, Caleb announced to Silas and Mrs Green that he was leaving that day and offered to pay them for his stay. The relief on Mrs Green's face was undisguised and in her relief she refused to accept one cent from him, even wishing the best of luck and saying that he was really a good man. It was very noticeable that she could not get out of the hotel fast enough, undoubtedly to inform Mrs Stein.

Like banks everywhere, the First National Bank in West Ridge kept very different hours from the rest of the working population. The stores and the timber mill opened their doors at six o'clock and by seven o'clock even the laziest of West Ridge's citizens were up and about. The owner of the saloon had been cleaning up since before six and was even serving a customer just after seven. The bank however, kept its shutters firmly closed until 9.30 and even when it did open, the clerk and the president of the bank did not appear to be in any hurry to deal with the eight or nine customers who were waiting.

Caleb met Sheriff Matt Brent as he slowly ambled from his office towards the bank, nodding briefly and grimly at Caleb. His manner did not seem to improve at the news that Caleb was leaving just as soon as he had collected the money.

Before the bank had opened, Caleb had collected his horse and had the offer of payment firmly refused by the deaf and dumb blacksmith. It appeared that nobody even wanted to touch his money for fear of becoming tainted.

James Pierce, the bank president, seemed to accept that Caleb was entitled to the money, although he insisted on various documents being signed by both Caleb and the sheriff before he would release it and even then he laboriously counted it out note for note and insisted that both Caleb and the sheriff did the same and then demanded two more signatures off each man.

James Pierce, the bank president, appeared to be a man of no opinions whatsoever as Caleb questioned him as to what he thought would happen next. In fact the only comment he did make, outside dealing with the money, was to inform the sheriff that the bank was closing early that day and that there would be very little money on the premises. Caleb did wonder just what was going to happen to the money in the safe, but he did not question the matter.

News had obviously spread around the town that Caleb had decided to leave and, far from being pleased at the prospect as he would have expected, the now quite sizeable crowd which had gathered outside the bank became quite hostile. There were cat-calls and remarks about his race, his colour and even his calling as a minister. Almost all accused him of running scared and deserting the town now that he had got his hands on the reward money.

Caleb bit his lip and kept his counsel as he mounted his horse. At first the crowd refused to move, some of the more vociferous amongst them demanding that he be held and handed over to Gill Weston in order to protect themselves. This call seemed to gain quite a lot of support and for a few moments the situation looked quite nasty. Caleb did notice that during this time Sheriff Matt Brent steadfastly remained inside the bank.

The crowd surged forward as the self-appointed ring-leader and spokesman, who noticeably kept himself well to the rear of the crowd, made another demand for the preacher to be held and handed over and Caleb, struggling to calm his horse which by this time was quite nervous, flung back the tails of his coat and rested his hand on his gun.

The effect was quite magical. The previously impenetrable wall of bodies suddenly parted, although the ring-leader was still urging everyone to seize the preacher and risk him using his gun. The crowd, however, whilst prepared to be whipped into a mild frenzy, were not prepared to chance their luck as far as testing the preacher's resolve with his guns. Caleb took his opportunity and urged his horse forward at a sudden gallop.

He had not had the time to think about it when it happened, but later he did wonder just what he would have done had the crowd tried to take him. He eventually came to the conclusion that he would probably have done nothing since it would have been rather a futile gesture. He just thanked God that the simple action of making the threat to use his guns had borne fruit.

His route took him from the town towards the forest and he wondered if it was such a wise move. It had been the original direction he had intended, but since he now knew that Gill Weston and his band were hiding out somewhere in the forest, the opposite direction would have been the more logical. However, he was now committed and could but hope that he did not meet the outlaws.

He had been travelling at a steady trot for about half an hour and, he estimated, six or seven miles when he caught sight of several riders heading towards him.

The trail had been winding steadily upwards for about a mile, past what appeared to be collection points for felled trees and, although he did not actually see anyone, there were unmistakable sounds of activity further into the forest. He eventually came to a ridge, still wooded either side, and it was from this ridge, that he looked down on the trail winding its way through the forest and alongside a small river. He saw the riders twice, once as they swept alongside the river and again a few moments later as they negotiated the twisting trail as it climbed upward.

Caleb was no coward and he had never knowingly ran out on a situation simply because he was frightened for his life. Like all men, there were times when he was frightened, even scared almost out of his wits, but he never knowingly used that as an excuse.

On this occasion, faced with the possibility of coming up against what appeared to be five men, he decided that prudence was the order of the day and pulled off the trail into the forest and hid himself and his horse behind some bushes to await the passing of the riders who, he had little doubt, were Gill Weston's men if not including Weston himself.

It seemed an eternity before the riders appeared on the trail now some fifty yards or so away and they seemed to be riding slowly to allow their horses to rest after the climb, but they soon passed and Caleb, to be certain that others were not behind, waited another five minutes or so before venturing back on to the trail.

He was about to make the quite steep descent when he suddenly found himself, without really thinking, turning his horse and heading back towards West Ridge.

No matter what the hostility was towards him from the townsfolk, he knew that it was his actions, legal or not, which had placed everyone in West Ridge in danger. As far as he was concerned even the loss of one innocent life because of anything he did was one life too many.

It was not that he had any noble ideas about giving himself up to the dubious mercies of Gill Weston, nothing was further from his mind, but he felt that he had to be on hand to give what assistance he could in the event of any reprisals. If nothing else he felt that he owed West Ridge that much. As to whether any action or interference on his part would be welcome, only time would tell, but he doubted that he would be welcomed with open arms.

The riders, five of them as he had thought, did not appear to be in any particular hurry, even laughing and joking amongst themselves and Caleb began to wonder if they even knew of the death of their fellow outlaws and even began to wonder if these men were anything to do with Gill Weston at all. More than once he had to stop and allow the men to get a little further ahead of him.

After a time, the one thing Caleb was certain of was that these men were not normal travellers. None of them had any of the trappings and accoutrements of travellers, no bedrolls, no water canteens and no cooking pots. No regular traveller was ever without these things, not even Caleb.

This of course indicated that he was in fact following some of Gill Weston's men if not the man himself. He had no way of knowing what Weston looked like. Sheriff Brent had claimed that he did not have a picture of Weston, but Caleb was now inclined to the belief that the sheriff simply did not want him to become involved.

Quite what he intended to do when the men did reach West Ridge, Caleb had no idea at all. Much would depend on what they did and even more on just how close he could get to them. As he remembered it, there was quite a high rise behind the town up to the tree line and the more gradual slope northward where the main trail ran. To the east, about half a mile from the town, ran a river whilst to the south the land was flat and open. He decided that the high ground behind the town would be the best place to observe what happened and he was quite certain that he could get close enough to be within range with his Winchester if need be.

As the men ahead neared West Ridge, their manner began to change, they became more alert and upright in their saddles and all checked their guns. For a moment Caleb was tempted to deal with them there and then and hope that they all had Wanted posters out on them. The only problem with that was that if they did not, or even one of them did not and was killed, Caleb himself would be charged with murder and it would be no defence to claim that he thought they were outlaws.

Half a mile out of town Caleb left the main trail and twisted his way through the trees towards where he had seen the rise and eventually he had found a very good position perched in the lower branches of a large tree but which gave him a clear view of most of the town and was definitely within range, although accuracy from that distance was likely to be a combination of good shooting and a large element of luck, with luck being the major factor.

The riders had arrived in West Ridge before Caleb had taken up position and were not to be seen. Their horses were tied to the hitching rail outside the saloon and he assumed that they were inside. He had to wait about ten minutes before anything started to happen.

The five men came out of the saloon and immediately split up, each in different directions and the reason for this very quickly became quite plain as each eventually returned to the area in front of the saloon herding a group of very frightened townsfolk. After a short time the men seemed satisfied and two stood each side of the gathering in the street, guns at the ready and prominently displayed whilst the fifth man mounted the boardwalk in front of the saloon and began to speak to the crowd.

Caleb's hearing was good, but it was not good enough to make out exactly what the man was saying, although he could have given a fairly accurate guess. His view of the man was somewhat restricted, only being able to catch occasional glimpses of his arm or legs as he moved about delivering his speech.

The man must have finished what he had to say as suddenly there were loud protests from the crowd, the most vociferous amongst them being Mrs Stein and from the odd word that drifted up to Caleb, he guessed that she was not being too polite to the men. After a short time Sheriff Matt Brent was ordered into the crowd to silence Mrs Stein. In the meantime two of the younger men were roughly pulled to one side, both protesting violently and manhandled across the street where they were spreadeagled against the wheels of a wagon and their arms and legs lashed to it.

The crowd once again protested loudly and it took a warning shot into the air to quell them. The man who had delivered the speech went to his horse and took off what looked like a coil of rope but which proved to be a bull-whip and he gave the onlookers a little demonstration of his prowess by cracking it a few times.

Caleb had seen a man bull-whipped once before and it had not been a pretty sight. The injuries had been so severe that the man had died in agony a few days later. Whippings were not an uncommon punishment but the use of the bull-whip was very rare. Normally the cane or the more slender horse whip were used and while being very painful, they inflicted less serious damage to the victim. Caleb, in his tree, had to think very quickly. The bull-whip meant almost certain death and he knew that he simply could not stand by and do nothing to help the victims.

One of the other men stepped forward and suddenly ripped the shirts off the young men strapped to the wheels and quickly stood to one side as the man with the whip cracked it a few more times and laughed loudly as he stepped ever closer to his victims.

Caleb did not remember actually raising his rifle to his shoulder but he found himself looking along the sight and lining it up with the man now strutting around in a very showman-like display which made a very difficult target. He cursed the man under his breath and willed him to stand still for just a few seconds. Eventually the man gave one final crack of his whip and stood to one side, flicked the whip out its full length along the ground, paused for a moment and then slowly drew his arm back.

As the whip began to snake forward at the end of its backward arc, Caleb squeezed the trigger of his Winchester. He was almost too late to save the young man from the first lash, but it just missed the man's back as it cracked across one of his boots. Even that probably hurt, but it would inflict no permanent damage and Caleb was already squeezing the trigger a second time.

The first shot had certainly found its target, but not quite as accurately as Caleb would have liked as the man, after falling to the ground, raised himself clutching at his upper arm. Caleb's second shot was even less accurate, splintering the wood of the wagon close to one of the young men.

Pure pandemonium broke loose as the crowd cried out in terror, fleeing along the street. The outlaws knew that there was nothing they could do, indeed three of them had dived for cover as soon as the first shot had echoed around.

Caleb realized that any further attempt to shoot the outlaws would be futile, he was too far away to be really effective.

However, he was satisfied that he had saved the young men—for the moment at least.

He caught a brief glimpse of the outlaws running to their horses as he slithered out of the tree and ran to his horse. In a way he cursed the luck that had made him return to West Ridge. Life would have been much easier had he not known anything about the aftermath of his killing of Coyne and Gates, but just as quickly he dismissed his selfish thoughts knowing that it would have preyed on his mind no matter what and he would have returned. At least this way he had been able to prevent a barbaric punishment even if only temporarily.

There was just one problem now, certainly not a new one as far as he was concerned; he had now transformed himself from hunter to hunted. Not only that, he had committed himself to the role of protector of the citizens of West Ridge. Whether they would immediately appreciate this change was most unlikely and in all probability they would not even be aware of it.

He had started something to which he knew there could be only two logical conclusions; the first was his own death, which might just be sufficient to appease Gill Weston and thus save the townsfolk from further punishment and the second conclusion would be the elimination of the outlaws. He certainly preferred the second option.

Whichever way it was destined to end, at that precise moment Caleb's first priority was to lose himself somewhere in the forest and avoid capture or death at the hands of the outlaws. The sound of hoof beats leaving West Ridge made him move just that little bit faster. He was no woodsman, more at home in the desert or plains and although he would have liked to have covered his tracks, he had neither the skill nor the time. All he could do was to trust to luck and hope to lose them.

Losing them was only part of his problem now. His other problem was, if he was to assume the role of protector of West Ridge, that he needed to know where the outlaws were hiding up and exactly how many of them there were. Once again he cursed himself for becoming involved and vowed to keep his nose out of things which would lead to situations like this in the future. He suddenly laughed out loud knowing that such a resolve would be broken almost immediately.

However, he could make all the resolutions he wanted, all of which would be of no use if he ended up dead.

FOUR

Caleb had had very little experience of travelling through forests other than by clearly defined trails and he had never given much thought to the difficulties involved. He very quickly discovered that trees alone were the least of the problems and that by far the most hazardous obstacles were largely unseen until he was on top of them.

Exposed tree roots were the chief hazard, followed by undergrowth which seemed to become more dense the further he went. Fallen trees and large branches were normally quite easy to negotiate although on more than one occasion his horse slipped on ancient branches and trees long buried beneath moss and fallen leaves. Eventually he found it easier and safer to dismount and lead his horse.

Shortly after he had started his trek

through the forest, he had heard the sounds of men pursuing him, but they seemed to have abandoned the idea and he wondered if this was because they knew that eventually he would have to emerge. The one thing that did surprise him was that he very quickly lost all sense of time and direction and more than once he was quite convinced that he had negotiated a particular obstacle before. After some time the going became a little easier and on finding a clear stream in an open glade, he and his horse rested.

With nowhere in particular to go and therefore having plenty of time on his hands, he opted to remain where he was for the moment and consider his position.

Behind him the ground appeared to rise quite steeply, although it was impossible to see how high it went due to the density of the trees but, although the slope looked quite slippery, he decided to climb it in the hope that at least he might be able to establish where he was in relation to the rest of the forest. Taking care to hobble his horse to prevent it wandering too far and taking his rifle with him just in case, he set off up the slope.

His first impression had not been wrong; the accumulation of fallen leaves, broken branches and thorn-covered undergrowth made his progress very slow and difficult and when he eventually did reach what was plainly the top of the slope about half an hour later, he sighed and shook his head, realizing that he had just wasted his time and effort as there was nothing to be seen except the underside of tree cover. He was about to turn and make the slippery descent back to his horse when the sound of someone chopping wood reached his ears on the slight wind.

The slope he had climbed seemed to level out and it was from this direction that the sound came. Logic told him that it was most unlikely that the outlaws would be chopping wood, other than possibly for their own use on a fire, but even then he thought it unlikely since there was no shortage of suitable fallen timber lying about. The only other people who would be chopping would be the lumberjacks employed by the timber company in West Ridge.

However, he was not too certain just what kind of reception he would receive from the lumberjacks. There had been one or two present in church the previous day and no doubt they had relayed the facts of what had happened to their companions. He had never had any dealings with such men although he had heard of them by repute and by all accounts they were a hard living, hard-drinking and hard working group of people who were apparently afraid of nothing and nobody.

He decided to follow the sound and he had not gone more that a hundred yards when the comparative peace and silence of the forest was suddenly shattered by the brief cry of "Timber!" followed almost immediately by loud cracks and groans as a tree crashed to the ground forcing its way through the dense foliage of surrounding trees.

The only trouble with this particular tree falling was that it came down exactly in line with him and, had he stood his ground, Caleb knew that he would almost certainly have been at least badly injured. As it was he managed to dive out of the path of the tree, ending up in a particularly dirty and smelly pool of stagnant water.

Caleb stood up, slowly wiping his hands down his coat in the realization of what he had landed in and silently cursed, in fact he was so intent on the condition of his clothes that he did not see or hear the man coming up behind him.

'Should've jumped the other way,' grinned the large man with a huge axe casually sloped across his broad shoulder. 'Ground's drier that side.'

'Thanks,' grunted Caleb, picking some unidentifiable vegetation from his coat, 'I'll remember that next time.'

Caleb was not a small man, but this lumberjack made even him look puny and the ease with which he handled the big axe as he slung it from his shoulder and sliced it through a branch of the now fallen tree made Caleb resolve not to become involved in a test of strength with him.

'You're the preacher from West Ridge

81

ain't you,' said the lumberjack more as a statement of fact rather than a question. 'I heard about you, about how you killed Coyne an' Gates. In fact there ain't been no other subject talked about since.'

'And does it bother you?' asked Caleb trying to wring some water out of his coat.

'Bother me?' The lumberjack seemed quite surprised at the question. 'Why the hell should it bother me?'

'Because it sure seemed to bother the folks in West Ridge,' said Caleb giving up on the idea of squeezing the water out of his clothes. 'When it happened I thought they didn't mind, it certainly didn't seem to bother them too much...'

The lumberjack took another swing with his axe and lopped off another stout branch. 'But then they realized that Gill Weston would take it out on them,' he interrupted. 'Sure, that's how things are round here.'

'And they were about to,' said Caleb. He went on to explain what had happened and how he came to be where he was now.

'You could hide out in this forest for a long time,' said the lumberjack who had announced his name as 'The Beast'! since his name was Frank Beaston. Caleb decided that 'The Beast' suited him very well.

'I can't really see me doing that,' said Caleb. 'I don't want to hang about any longer than I have to, but I feel that I owe it to West Ridge to help since I appear to have caused them some trouble.'

'Don't see what you can do,' said The Beast in a matter-of-fact way. 'Gill Weston seems to have the upper hand around here.'

Caleb looked at the huge frame of The Beast and could not really believe that anyone, outlaw or not, could ever have the upper hand with men like him.

'You too?' he asked.

The Beast laughed and swung his axe to lop off another stout branch. 'He likes to think so,' laughed The Beast. The way he said it confirmed in Caleb's mind that the lumberjacks were probably their own men. 'He don't bother us so we don't bother him,' continued The Beast. 'It seems to suit us all.'

'But not the folk in West Ridge,' Caleb pointed out.

'That's their problem,' grunted The Beast, swinging his axe yet again at a branch, although this one took two blows to sever it. 'Folk in town like our money well enough, but they don't seem too keen on mixin' too much, 'specially when it comes to their women.'

Caleb smiled and nodded. In some ways his sympathy was with the citizens of West Ridge. He could well imagine the demands placed upon the female population by burly lumberjacks with money in their pockets and little to spend it on.

'That is one problem I have no intention of becoming embroiled in, but I still feel that since I have created a problem it is up to me to put things right. Where is this Gill Weston camped out?'

The big man carefully placed the axe on the toe of his boot, leaned on the handle and stared, almost mockingly, into the preacher's eyes. Both men held each other's gaze for a few moments before The Beast gave a cynical laugh and picked up his axe again.

'Now if I was you, Reverend,' he said slowly, 'I'd forget all about it. Weston's holed up somewheres even the cavalry couldn't get into nor get him out of. Not only that, if he catches anyone within a mile his solution is quick an' sure—he kills 'em. I know, I seen three other men, bounty hunters they were, who tried their luck an' they ended up as wolf meat.'

'I'm not the cavalry,' Caleb pointed out.

'Neither were the bounty hunters,' responded The Beast. 'I do hear that there's been others who've tried an' every one of 'em has failed. There was even a marshal with a few deputies about a year ago. They wasn't killed but they gave up on the idea.'

Now if there was one thing guaranteed to make Caleb Black dig his heels in and tackle any problem, it was the assertion that such a thing was impossible. In his youth he had been told that it was impossible for him to receive a good education because of the colour of his skin—he had proved everyone wrong. When he had joined the army, albeit under some duress, he had been told that he would never make an officer—he had left with the rank of lieutenant even if it was attained in a purely black regiment. Becoming a minister had been easier, black ministers were quite common although their ministries were normally confined to black congregations. In that respect he had yet to prove otherwise, although he had often preached to largely white or even wholly white congregations—as in West Ridge—but that was through force of circumstance rather than total acceptance. This assertion that it would be impossible for him to penetrate Gill Weston's camp simply made him all the more determined.

'I'll think about it,' he said, rather tamely he thought. 'Right now I could do with somewhere to hide up for a while an' think things out.'

'Hidin' up's no problem,' grinned The

Beast, sweeping his arm around. 'There's miles of it.'

'I was thinking of somewhere a little more comfortable,' said Caleb. 'Such as your camp.'

The Beast did not appear to be surprised and nodded briefly. 'I guess you'd be as safe there as anywhere. Very occasionally we get one or two of Weston's men passin' through, although it ain't often they stop. I suppose they just like to let us know they're keepin' an eye on things.'

'Sounds good to me,' said Caleb. 'How do I get there?'

'You say you're horse is down the hill?' The Beast nodded in that direction and Caleb nodded in confirmation. 'Just follow the creek upstream, it passes right through. This time of day there ain't goin' to be nobody there 'ceptin' old Cripple Dyke. Just tell him The Beast says it's OK though.'

'Cripple Dyke?' queried Caleb.

The Beast smiled. 'He don't mind that name, we all got names like that, none of us ever gets called by our real names.

Most of us don't know the real name of the fellers we've been workin' with for years. He's called Cripple Dyke 'cos he got himself crippled when a dyke collapsed on him somewheres up in Canada. I think his real name is somethin' like Smith.'

Caleb grinned and decided that, as in the case of The Beast, the name was probably most apt. The Beast went on to explain that Cripple Dyke had been a lumberjack, one of the best The Beast assured, and that he had never been able to settle to any other life since his accident and was now employed by the lumberjacks as camp boss and cook, with the emphasis on cooking.

Caleb left The Beast to continue stripping the fallen tree of its branches and returned to the creek and his horse, slithering down the steep slope and reaching the creek far quicker than he had departed.

His horse was unhobbled and led upstream. He could have ridden, the going was easy enough, but he decided that since he had plenty of time, it would be best spent considering his next move. The impression he had received from The Beast was that the camp was not very far upstream, but in the event it proved to be at least three miles and three miles in a dense forest is a very long way.

Somehow Caleb had expected the camp to be within a stockade. Bears were quite common in the area and notoriously curious, but that was not what he found. It appeared that each man was responsible for providing his own accommodation and this ranged from small but seemingly well constructed log cabins to rough-looking tents. The only protection offered was that it was in a hollow surrounded by large rocks. The creek ran through the centre of the camp and the first indication that there was any real organization came with the unmistakable odour of human excrement and waste.

Coming in the direction he did, meant that Caleb approached the camp on its downstream section which was the latrine area and waste dump. The fact that there were bears about was confirmed quite suddenly and frighteningly when a large, brown body suddenly rose out of the waste dump, chewing on what appeared to be a piece of meat, and stared unblinkingly at Caleb.

He had never been that close to a wild bear before, although he had seen and touched a few who were kept captive and used by circus performers. He had also seen a few caged animals which were kept purely for fighting or bearbaiting, a barbaric sport in his opinion in which he always dearly wanted the dogs to lose.

The animal did not make any attempt to charge at Caleb but he left nothing to chance and quickly led his horse, now quite terrified, past the dump and the latrines into the main camp, where he was greeted by a large, rather bent man who plainly had difficulty walking, who looked at him with a mixture of curiosity and contempt.

'There's a bear out there!' blustered Caleb.

'Ben!' snapped Cripple Dyke. 'That ain't

no bear, that's Ben.'

'Well he sure looked like a bear to me,' said Caleb.

Cripple Dyke grinned toothlessly at his visitor. 'Oh, he's a bear all right, that's as plain as the nose on your face but we calls him Ben on account of him bein' big like Big Ben—that's a clock somewheres in England from what I hear. Leastways Lord Jim says it is an' he ought to know, he's an Englishman.'

'Doesn't he bother you?' asked Caleb.

'The bear or Lord Jim?' Cripple Dyke laughed at his own joke. 'Naw, Ben ain't no problem. In fact he's a good thing. That dump is his territory an' he makes sure no other bears come anywhere near.'

Caleb was still not convinced that the bear was harmless or that he was a good thing to have around, but he accepted Cripple Dyke's word for it.

'The Beast told me to come here,' he explained. 'I met up...'

'That's good enough for me,' grunted Cripple Dyke. 'I was sorta expectin' you anyhow. You're that preacher they call

Caleb Black ain't you.' This was not a question it was a statement of fact. 'Good name too, Black. Anyhow, they've already been out here lookin' for you, 'course I told 'em I hadn't seen nor heard of you, which I hadn't then since you only just turned up. Anyhow, they said I was to get word to 'em if you did show up.'

'I take it you mean Gill Weston,' said Caleb.

'Now who the hell else would I be talkin' about?' said Cripple Dyke spitting an evil looking wad of something on to the ground.

'Possibly the sheriff from West Ridge,' volunteered Caleb.

Cripple Dyke spat on the ground again and sneered. 'He'd be lost past the first tree. We don't see folk from West Ridge up here 'ceptin' the clerk from the mill on pay days, which is every two weeks. That's when we all hit town an' when I say hit, I mean hit. Folk think we're animals an' they do their best to keep their wives an' daughters locked up an' out of our way...' He grinned knowingly. 'Don't make much difference though. Some of them women are just as hot for it as we are. While one keeps their menfolk occupied there's others keepin' their women occupied!' He laughed coarsely and spat again. 'Anyhow, I been told to let Weston know if you showed up.'

'And are you going to?' asked Caleb.

Cripple Dyke grinned and chewed hard on something in his toothless mouth and looked thoughtful. 'Maybe I will, maybe I won't,' he said. 'It all depends.'

'Depends on what?' asked Caleb.

'On how I'm feelin',' grinned Cripple Dyke. 'Mind you, I could be made to feel a whole lot better'n I do right now.'

'And how do I make you feel better?' asked Caleb, sensing that demands were about to be made upon the money he had gained in West Ridge. He was not wrong.

'I hear tell you did pretty well off the collection plate an' that you collected one hundred an' fifty dollars for killin' Coyne an' Gates. Now it seems to me that if Gill Weston gets his hands on you all that money ain't goin' to do you no good at all...' Caleb had to agree with the logic so far. 'Now I ain't a greedy man, but bein' like I am...'—he raised a twisted leg and showed a hand with only two fingers—'I ain't like the others an' can earn good money, I have to do this job which is OK, but it don't pay the same. I used to earn good money, as good as anyone before my accident, one of the best I was. I wasn't called Cripple Dyke in them days though, The Beaver I was then on account of I was the best at ridin' logs down river.' He paused and thought for a moment. 'I'd say a hundred dollars'd make me forget all about them bein' here, or you for that matter.'

This was what Caleb had expected. 'Twenty-five!' he countered.

Cripple Dyke spat on to the ground with obvious contempt. 'Hundred!' he insisted.

Caleb sighed, realizing that he would have to raise the price. 'Fifty!' he offered. 'That's all, no more. It's fifty, take it or leave it an' I'll chance you telling Weston.'

Cripple Dyke looked hard at the preacher for a moment, spat another obscene wad on to the ground and then grinned. 'OK, fifty it is,' he agreed, stretching out his hand.

Actually Caleb had been prepared to go a little higher and was slightly surprised that Cripple Dyke had given in so easily. He realized that the out-stretched hand was not to shake hands on the deal, but in expectation of the money. Caleb sighed and took his money folder out of his coat pocket, deliberately turned away from the camp boss and counted out fifty dollars in ten-dollar bills.

The money was eagerly snatched out of Caleb's hand and stuffed into a shirt pocket without even being counted. The man turned and walked towards what was obviously the kitchen and mess area of the camp, a structure consisting of a series of stout poles and a roof. There were no sides except for the far end behind which was what must have been Cripple Dyke's own accommodation.

'Where do I go?' asked Caleb, tethering his now calmed horse to one of the poles.

'The Beast's cabin is over there,' replied Cripple Dyke, waving his two-fingered hand towards a log cabin perched on top of a mound. 'If he's invited you here it's up to him to see you've got a bed, not me.'

'I'll wait until he comes back,' said Caleb, not wishing to push his welcome too far. 'In the meantime have you anywhere I can clean up myself an' these clothes, oh, and for fifty dollars I think a meal ought to be included.'

Cripple Dyke looked at the preacher almost in astonishment.

'Clean yourself up?' he queried. 'You mean a bath or somethin', with real soap an' hot water?'

'What else?' grinned Caleb.

Cripple Dyke still looked amazed. 'But it ain't Saturday mornin'! Nobody bothers with washin' or bathin' 'cept on Saturday mornin' after pay out. We wouldn't bother then either if it warn't for the women. They seem to like it when we goes into town all clean an' smellin' nice.'

'I like to bathe a little more frequently

than that,' said Caleb. 'I ended up in a foul-smelling pool trying to avoid a tree and my clothes stink.'

Cripple Dyke sniffed and shook his head. 'You smell all right to me.' He suddenly grinned. 'Anyhow, a feller your colour shouldn't need to wash too often, dirt don't show so easy as it does on a white skin.'

'I can still feel it though,' said Caleb, not insulted by this remark. 'And I can still smell my clothes.'

Cripple Dyke shrugged and pointed towards another open sided structure a few yards away. 'There's hip baths in there,' he said. 'There's probably some soap lyin' about, there usually is.' He pointed towards a large, steaming cauldron alongside the cooking range. 'You'll have to carry the water from there. There's a jug there somewhere. On Saturday mornin's, when we're goin' to town, I light a couple of boilers in the wash hut, but they just ain't needed 'ceptin' every two weeks.'

Caleb thanked him for the information, went to the wash hut and found a piece of soap, very hard and cracked, emptied some leaves out of one of the baths and then stripped down to his longjohns which, when new some months ago, had been white but were now a distinctly dirty grey colour. He would not normally have chosen white for such a garment, but that had been all that was available at the time.

It took twelve large jugs of water to fill the bath to his satisfaction and then he obeyed Cripple Dyke's instruction to replace the water from the stream. By the time he did sink into his bath the temperature had cooled somewhat but it was still most welcome.

His clothes were washed in the same water he bathed in, which was something he usually did and, grudgingly, Cripple Dyke produced a large, very rough towel. Caleb had taken a spare set of underclothes from his saddle bag and appeared alongside Cripple Dyke in nothing but these and his boots. Cripple Dyke looked him up and down for a moment, made some comment about him looking just like any other man and then ladled some stew on to a plate which he set at the nearest table.

'Stew!' he announced. 'It's always stew. Sometimes it's deer meat, sometimes it's goat an' it's even been bear, but it's always stew. I tried givin' 'em a proper roast meal once, you know, proper roast meat, potatoes, vegetables an' things like that, but they almost threw it at me an' demanded stew. So, that's what they get.'

'Very nourishing too,' said Caleb, prodding the mixture with his knife as if expecting something to suddenly rise out of it and bite him.

Cripple Dyke might not have been well up on the presentation aspect of his cooking, but the looks belied the taste and Caleb discovered that it was just about the best stew he had ever tasted. The meat turned out to be deer, since that was the most plentiful source of meat, followed by wild goat and bear. He was thankful that bear was not on the menu today.

Afterwards he hung his clothes out to dry, unsaddled his horse and waited for the return of the lumberjacks.

FIVE

It was almost dusk before the first of the lumberjacks returned to camp, all staring at Caleb suspiciously but most saying nothing, more interested in satisfying their hunger, although there were various comments and obscenities questioning the arrival of the preacher on the scene.

Shortly after the first group of lumberjacks arrived, the sound of chains being dragged heralded the arrival of four enormous work horses, obviously well cared for by two men, not quite as large as the lumberjacks, who each led a pair. Behind each pair trailed long chains attached to what looked like a yoke, except that it was not worn by the animals.

The horses were led across the creek and under the cover of another sideless structure which Caleb had noticed but had not asked about. The size of the horses was in keeping with the size of the men who cut the timber, anything smaller would have looked very odd.

Eventually The Beast arrived, threw his axe down at the feet of the preacher and laughed. 'I hear they been lookin' for you,' he boomed. 'Lord Jim an' The Bear told me they'd seen 'em.'

Caleb assumed, quite rightly, that The Bear did not refer to the bear called Ben on the rubbish heap. 'And I'll bet that they told them to report if I did show up.' He sincerely hoped that this did not mean a further drain on his finances.

'Somethin' like that,' nodded The Beast. 'You eaten?'

'Earlier on,' said Caleb, 'but I could sure eat somethin' right now. That's just about the best stew I ever tasted.'

The Beast laughed. 'Just about the only thing that he does real good. Stew an' dumplin's an' fruit duff.'

It appeared that the fruit duff was still in the process of being cooked when Caleb had eaten, but now he was ready to try anything. The stew and dumplings lived up to expectation and the fruit duff was equally good. Afterwards, the lumberjacks became a little more sociable and gathered round Caleb. Three of them introduced themselves as having been at his service, although he did not recognize them. As far as he was concerned all lumberjacks looked exactly the same.

No demands were made upon his finances and, although tempted, Caleb did not mention that Cripple Dyke had received payment. That night he slept in reasonable comfort in The Beast's small cabin. During the evening he had learned the names of almost everyone at the camp, although there was no way he could remember them all, but a few stood out.

There was Lord Jim, the Englishman who spoke in a very funny way although he insisted that everyone else spoke peculiarly and not he. There was The Bear who, like The Beast, was certainly not a man to be tangled with—not that any of them were, it was just that one or two looked more formidable than the others. There was Paddy the Fox and Paddy the Skunk, apparently brothers from Ireland. The Monkey, so named because of the speed he could climb trees, came from Spain and The Piper, a Scotsman who took his bagpipes everywhere.

The Piper insisted on giving a demonstration of his prowess with that strange instrument, a feat apparently not appreciated by his fellow lumberjacks nor Caleb and most certainly not by Ben who made loud protesting noises from the waste dump. In fact only the horses appeared unaffected, including Caleb's horse.

He also learned that none of the lumberjacks owned a horse and that between them they only had two rifles, both used for hunting. Caleb did ask about the safety of the payroll coming out all this way and he was assured that even Gill Weston dare not touch that particular payroll. He could well see why Gill Weston did not try to intercept it. Thirty or so burly lumberjacks rampaging through the forest would be more than any man dare tackle.

The following morning, as dawn broke, everyone sat down for a surprisingly good breakfast of porridge—a little thick for Caleb's taste—steak, hash-browns and eggs. Then the men began to wander off to fell even more timber.

Caleb had considered his position and had decided that even if he could not get into the outlaws' camp, he would at least like to know where it was and just what he was up against. Somewhat reluctantly The Beast agreed to show him the way, stressing that whatever happened, Caleb was on his own.

There was little point in taking his horse, but Cripple Dyke seemed reluctant to have it kept in camp, pointing out that should Weston's men return, which they may well do, the horse would stand out like a beacon and be almost impossible to explain away.

So it was that The Beast and Caleb made their way northward with Caleb's horse in tow. The Beast did not seem too worried about meeting any of the outlaws, saying that they kept mainly to the regular tracks and only rarely ventured into the forest proper, which was the way he and Caleb were now going.

Caleb's biggest worry was would he be able to find his way back to the lumberjacks' camp. Even with The Beast guiding him, his sense of direction had almost completely deserted him and time too seemed to pass at a faster rate.

Eventually they came to a small river where The Beast stopped on a small ridge above the narrow valley and pointed across. As far as Caleb could see there was nothing to distinguish the opposite bank from the one they were standing on and the river could easily have been the creek flowing through the camp, but he knew that it was not, if only because The Beast told him so.

'Just keep followin' your nose,' said The Beast. 'The ground rises for about half a mile, but it ain't too bad. It brings you out on to a high, steep ridge with maybe a drop of three or four hundred feet. The valley you'll be lookin' down on leads up to Weston's camp. All I know about the place is what I've seen from a distance an' what I've heard. Accordin' to Lord Jim, he strayed up there once an' came across the camp. He says it's near a high rock in the middle of the valley. Says it looks like a rhino horn, standin' about two hundred feet...'

'Rhino horn?' queried Caleb.

'That's what I said,' grinned The Beast. 'He reckons it's some sort of animal with a horn stickin' out of its nose. Says he's seen one once when he was aboard a slaver in Africa. It don't mean a thing to me either, but I guess it must look like some kinda horn.'

'I've heard of a lot of things,' said Caleb, 'but an animal with a horn stickin' out of its nose? I've met a few sailors before an' it seems to me they're full of tales that can't be true. They have a very vivid imagination.'

The Beast shrugged. 'Lord Jim don't strike me as no liar,' he said in defence of his fellow lumberjack. 'Just 'cos you an' me ain't seen it don't mean it don't exist.

Have you ever seen your God?'

Caleb looked at his guide for a moment and was seriously considering taking him to task at what he perceived as being close to blasphemy in hinting that the God of Caleb was not his God. However, common sense prevailed in that he doubted very much if The Beast was a man capable of philosophical or deep theological argument—and the knowledge that one blow of one of those huge fists could bring such discussion to a rapid conclusion.

'Perhaps not,' he said very tamely. 'Is this as far as you go?'

'I've come further than I intended already,' replied The Beast. 'From here on you're on your own. Just remember the rhino horn an' the camp bein' close to it.' The big man turned and, slinging his huge axe casually and easily across his shoulder, started back the way they had come. 'Don't know what you mean to do,' he called back, 'but I'd say this is the last time I'll be seein' you, 'ceptin' maybe findin' your body somewheres.'

Caleb vaguely remembered saying something about being able to look after himself, but suddenly he was alone. The Beast had simply disappeared, swallowed up in the dark underbelly of the forest. For a few moments he felt very alone and, for the first time, very vulnerable. The Beast had let it be known that in his opinion he, Caleb, was completely mad, but then he also made it plain that he considered all preachers to be mad.

Caleb too was beginning to wonder if The Beast's assessment did contain a large element of truth. Here he was, set on a mission which in all probability would prove impossible and for a cause which was not of his making or even concern, other than that he had aggravated that situation somewhat. However, better judgement lost the day and he set off on his self-appointed mission.

The Beast's assertion that the going up to the ridge was not too bad certainly bore little resemblance to Caleb's idea of not too bad. It was steep, slippery and full of obstacles. However, he eventually found himself at the top and looking down on a valley about half a mile wide cutting through sheer rock walls at least 400 hundred feet high.

What The Beast had failed to tell him was how to get down into that valley as it appeared he needed to. A brief survey each side of where he was revealed nothing. The walls of rock were sheer for as far as the eye could see. There was not even a regular path or track for him to follow, the only indication being what looked like a deer track. With little else to follow, he followed this although he quickly discovered that it was a goat track as he scattered a feeding group all of whom seemed to throw themselves over the edge of the cliff. A brief look down showed that the animals were running along the sheer rock almost as if they were on the level.

After a very short distance further, he decided that the track was too close to the edge for comfort and moved his horse, which he had chosen to ride, further in among the trees whilst making sure that he kept the valley within sight.

About fifteen minutes after scattering the goats, Caleb became aware that he was travelling downhill, quite gradually but definitely downhill and, in confirmation, he looked over the edge and found that the drop was now only about half what it had been, although it was still a long drop. Ten minutes later, without warning, he found himself coming out on to a boulder-strewn river bed.

If anything, it was harder going along the river bed than through the forest and all sense of time simply vanished. It was not until he stopped to allow his horse to rest that he looked at his watch and realized that it was now more than four hours since he had left the lumberjacks' camp.

He began to believe that The Beast had sent him on some sort of fool's errand, probably in the hope or knowledge that having gone this far he would not turn back. It was at that moment that Caleb decided that if he had been sent on a fool's errand, he certainly would not be turning back and probably more than half of him hoped that this was the case.

The one thing he was quite certain of was that if the outlaw camp was indeed somewhere up here, there must be a much easier way in and out. He had lost all sense of direction; as far as he was concerned where he was now could be a hundred miles from West Ridge or a mile. He had the feeling that north was ahead of him, upstream, but he was not even certain of that since the sun had been blocked out by the mountains rising high into the sky on either side, behind and even ahead.

Shortly after he resumed his now wearisome journey, he came across a sharp bend in the river and was forced to cross to the other bank to avoid what looked a very deep pool. He had no doubts that the horse could swim but that was one of the few things that he could not do and did not want to try.

Suddenly, round the bend, standing majestically in the centre of the valley, which had by this time narrowed to little more than 400 hundred yards or so, was what was plainly the rhino horn The Beast had mentioned.

It was indeed a horn-shaped rock with a distinct curve on one side bending sharply inwards which gave the impression that the pointed top was about to fall over at any moment. Caleb's first reaction was that if that was the shape of a rhino horn then it must be a very peculiar animal indeed. His next thought was to question if his approach had been witnessed and to avoid the possibility, if it had not, he moved up the side of the river-bank to hide amongst a clump of trees.

It was a good half-hour before Caleb decided that his arrival must have gone unnoticed, during which time he had been weighing up the options before him. The Beast had not said which side of the river the outlaw camp was, but it seemed quite obvious that it could not be on the far side from where he now was, since there was a sheer cliff rising about 300 feet and stretching along the river as far as he could see.

The side he was now on, although high and steep, was tree covered and offered a way up. Taking his horse appeared completely out of the question so, suitably armed with hand-guns and his rifle, he slowly edged his way along the river-bed, keeping as close in as possible, until he found a place which seemed to offer the best and easiest way up.

The climb must have taken him the best part of half an hour although the actual distance covered was little more than 3 or 400 hundred yards. Eventually he found himself on relatively level, tree-covered ground with a fairly well-defined track. He followed the track upstream for a short distance and suddenly found himself looking down on to treeless, almost fortress-like rocks, roughly forming a circular basin some fifty or so feet above the river.

At first there was little to be seen except the occasional flight of birds but, quite unexpectedly, from almost directly below where he was standing, two riders appeared following what Caleb now realized was a track through the scattered rocks. As the riders reached the centre of the fortress, they dismounted and almost immediately two other men appeared, this time on foot.

Caleb could not help but smile with satisfaction as he suddenly began to notice things that had somehow remained hidden before. Little things such as a thin plume of smoke, something he was quite certain would have stood out like a beacon to a trained woodsman. Horses, which until that moment had remained camouflaged against the brown and grey rocks, suddenly became so obvious that he seriously questioned why he had not been able to distinguish them before. The one thing he was now quite certain of was that he had found the outlaws' camp.

Having discovered their camp was one thing, that was, after all, what he had set out to do; what to do with that knowledge was an entirely different matter. He was one man against many, exactly how many was unknown, but there were plainly too many and too well protected. He sat and watched the comings and goings for some time, trying to calculate just how many men there were. He thought he could make out seven individuals, but since they were never all in one place at the same time, it was impossible to be certain. He could have counted some men twice and it was just as possible that there were others who had yet to show themselves.

He was just about resigned to the fact that the exercise he had undertaken was an arduous waste of time, when two men he definitely had not seen before, came from the direction of the river leading a horse.

It took a few moments for Caleb to realize, to his horror, that the horse they were leading was his. His blood seemed to freeze in his veins and he found himself looking about, suddenly hearing noises which had been ever-present, in a different light. Each sound now assumed a new significance as he imagined outlaws closing in on him.

The scene below had now changed from leisurely to almost frantic. Voices were raised and plainly orders were being given as men snatched up rifles and ran towards the forest. Caleb had no need to wonder who or what they were after.

The urgency of the situation suddenly hit Caleb and he started to run deeper into the forest; although he was running blind with all sense of direction having deserted him completely, he did have enough sense to realize that going back to the river would lead to certain capture and probably death. His one thought at that moment was to lose his pursuers in the forest as he had before.

There seemed to be a lot of noise and it took him some time to realize that most of that noise was being made by him and was probably acting as a guide to the men he knew to be following. He stopped, panting heavily and listened although at first he was unable to hear anything but the pounding of his heart and his own gasps for breath.

Slowly his breathing became easier and his ears more attuned to the sounds around him and he realized that he was on his own; there did not seem to be anyone in hot pursuit although he was well aware that they could not be far away. The outlaws had the advantage in that they had had the time to become acclimatized to the forest, they knew where they were and which way they were going, he did not.

He moved on, slowly and quietly this time, his rifle clasped in his hand ready to use in an instant should it prove necessary. Once or twice he had to hide behind trees or bushes as sudden movements came and went ahead of him. All of these movements proved to be deer, all except one which, although he never actually saw it, he was convinced was a bear.

He had heard about bears, mostly how dangerous they were and although he thought the accounts were often very much embellished to suit the role of the particular person relating the account, he had no wish to test his theory at that moment.

What seemed like hours later but in fact was no more than thirty minutes since overlooking the outlaw camp, Caleb quite suddenly and somehow unexpectedly, found himself walking out of the forest on to a well defined and well used track. Quite why he was surprised he did not know, logic told him that there must be at least one trail through the forest leading to the outlaw camp if nowhere else. He looked up into the sky hoping to see the sun but, although it was plainly quite bright, there was plenty of cloud cover and, both to his left and right, high mountains towered above him, ahead and behind there was nothing to be seen except trees.

He sighed and shook his head in disgust as he resolved that should he somehow survive this situation, he needed to become more acquainted with the art of telling which direction was which even without the aid of the sun. As it was, there did not appear to be even any shadows which indicated the position of the sun with the result that he quite frankly had no idea which direction was which and he knew that such knowledge could make the difference between getting caught and staying free and therefore the difference between life and death.

He did, however, have enough sense to

realize that he could not keep to the trail since it was certain to be only a matter of time before the outlaws would be riding along it. Mentally tossing a coin to decide which direction to go, he moved back into the protection offered by the trees and went to his right with the trail on his left hoping that it was the correct choice.

Caleb was faced with another decision he would rather not have had to make; he looked down into a narrow but deep gully along which water rushed over jagged rocks and fallen tree trunks. The trail he had been closely following veered left along the top of the gully and appeared to be the most logical way for him to go. However, at that moment logic was not too high on Caleb's schedule, had it been he would not have allowed himself to be in the position he now was.

He turned into the forest, following the course of the gully in the hope of finding a way to cross but the further he went the wider and deeper the gully appeared to become and his surroundings also seemed to become more hostile and difficult. Eventually he had to admit defeat when faced with a high, slippery drop of about fifty feet. He turned and made his way back to the trail.

Looking at the log bridge across the gully, Caleb was filled with a sense of foreboding. There was no obvious reason for the feeling and it was rare for him to feel that way, but this time it was very strong.

He had followed the trail for about half a mile, all the time making his way through the cover of the trees alongside it and had come to the bridge. It consisted of about ten stout tree trunks stretched across what appeared to be the narrowest section of the gully, but it was not the actual bridge which filled him with foreboding, indeed it appeared very solid. He could not explain his feeling and there definitely was nothing to make him think that anything was amiss.

He could, of course, avoid the bridge altogether and continue to follow the gully, but at that point the ground appeared to be rising rapidly and looked as though it simply ended up at the base of the high mountain now towering above the trees. For some time he stayed where he was, looking and listening although he could neither see nor hear anything unusual and there was no evidence that anyone was waiting for him. Eventually, after looking at his watch and seeing that there was little more than two hours until sunset, he decided to remain where he was and cross the bridge in the dark.

That idea might have been the one sound judgement that Caleb had made for several days and had he been able to wait he might very well have reached West Ridge in safety. However, as with most things, fate had decreed that crossing the bridge was not something that could be delayed until it suited Caleb.

He had settled himself into the bole of a tree with a view of the bridge and found himself beginning to doze off when suddenly and terrifyingly, he was jerked back into reality by low rumbling noises close behind him.

Rifle in hand, ready to shoot, Caleb looked round the tree, still sitting, to find himself staring into the mean, brown eyes of a huge bear. At least it seemed like a huge bear since at that point the animal was no more than three feet away from him. For a moment it was not too certain who was the more surprised, Caleb or the bear but it was the bear which acted first and decisively as it lunged towards the preacher.

Caleb did not remember if he shot the animal or not, his feeling was that he had not. However, he did remember screaming out and racing towards the bridge with the bear in full pursuit. What happened next he never did find out but he had vague memories of at least two shots being fired followed by the sensation of falling into a deep abyss, although he knew he had crossed the gully...

SIX

The pain in Caleb's head was momentarily replaced by a sudden pain in his chest, seemingly caused by a huge tree crashing down on him. At least that was the vision which flashed through his mind, but a distant voice seemed to indicate otherwise. He was quite certain that the disembodied voice was ordering him to stand up, which at that moment was an act completely beyond his capabilities. The tree crashed down again and was again followed by the command to get up.

The nearest Caleb came to getting off the ground was to force open his eyes, just in time to see a boot descending towards his body. There was nothing he could do to avoid the blow but he did manage to grit his teeth and suppress a cry of pain. At least he thought he had, he could not be too certain.

'He's come to,' someone announced, presumably the owner of the boot. 'His eyes are open.'

'Not for much longer if you keep kicking me!' said Caleb, but again he was uncertain if the words had only formed in his mind and not his mouth. Whichever way it was, a face suddenly appeared above him, grinned evilly, spat a wad of something close to his head, leered at him again and then spoke to someone nearby. What was said was beyond Caleb's capacity to hear and he really did not care.

Suddenly he felt someone grab him under his arms and then he was unceremoniously hauled to his feet. That was the easy part, the hard part was retaining his upright stance without assistance. Eventually his brain stopped spinning around inside his head for long enough and he remained upright, although plainly swaying considerably.

He was tempted to ask the inevitable question, 'What happened?', but even in his state of semi stupor, he realized that it was a futile question. The memory of the bear chasing him flashed through his mind and he did wonder, briefly, if the animal had reached him first.

'Maybe we should've let the bear have him,' said a nearby voice. 'I ain't never seen a man ripped to death by a bear; I hear they make a real mess.'

That seemed to answer the question of whether or not the bear had reached him first. Caleb brought his eyes into focus and stared at the man nearest to him. 'I don't know whether to thank you or not,' he said, trying to smile, but knowing that he probably did nothing more than leer.

'Thank us for what?' asked the man.

'Saving me from the bear,' said Caleb.

'Maybe Seth was right,' replied the man, 'maybe we should've let it have you. Only reason I didn't was 'cos I'm curious about you.'

Caleb raised a hand to feel his head, rubbed his fingers through something wet, looked at his hand, now stained with blood, and smiled sardonically.

'Unless I'm very much mistaken, that's blood...!' He showed his hand to the man.

'Now since the bear seemingly didn't get to me, I'd say that was caused by a bullet. It seems a strange kind of logic to save me from a wild animal and shoot me at the same time.'

The man grinned. 'Sure, that shot was meant to kill you, there's no denyin' that an' I sure wouldn't've lost no sleep about it if you had been killed. Seth here was all for puttin' a bullet through your head when we found you was still alive, but I got to thinkin' that there were a few things I wanted to know.'

'Why stop the bear?' Caleb asked.

'I guess that was a gut reaction,' said the man. 'Somebody fired without thinkin'. Don't know if we hit the bear or not, don't think so, he just ran off.'

'I'm pleased for the bear,' said Caleb. 'As to answering your questions, I'm not too sure that I have anything to tell you or that I am capable of giving a coherent answer at this moment.'

The man laughed and shook his head. 'Reverend, you is wastin' your time usin' big words like that around here. We ain't none of us had proper schoolin' an' there's only one left what can read an' write.'

'Big words?' said Caleb, slightly mystified. 'Oh, I see, you mean "coherent"? That means understandable, making sense.'

'If'n you say so,' grinned the man. 'All I'm sayin' is if you want to say somethin', make sure you use words we all understand.'

'If'n you say so,' mocked Caleb, although it seemed lost on the man. 'From the way you're talking I'd say your name was Gill Weston, leader of this outlaw band I've heard so much about.'

The man seemed impressed. 'Sure, that's me,' he said, proudly. 'And you're that black preacher what turned up in West Ridge an' killed two of my best men.'

'That doesn't say much for the others,' said Caleb, again mockingly which again went over Weston's head.

'Yeh,' continued Weston. 'Gates an' Coyne was real useful, they was good with a gun an' they could read an' write. Not only that but they could use numbers too, you know, all that multiplyin' an' dividin' stuff. Even Frank ain't too good at numbers but he can read an' write.'

Caleb refrained from asking just who Frank was since he was not really interested and he had no doubt that, given time, he would discover who he was. From what Caleb had heard, Gill Weston had just broken one of his own rules in not killing the intruder there and then, which indicated to Caleb that the man was fallible. Whether or not the fallibility of Gill Weston would or could be of any future benefit was rather uncertain, but for the moment at least he was still alive if rather bruised and sore.

'What now?' he asked.

'We take you back,' said Weston. 'It ain't far, the walk'll do you good.' He laughed. 'Maybe it'll make you more...what was that word you used? Coherent! Yeh, that was it. Maybe it'll make you more coherent.'

The walk, surprisingly shorter than Caleb had expected, did help to clear his mind and ease his joints. His guns had been taken from him, although he still wore his crossed gunbelts. His rifle now appeared to have become the property of the man called Seth. His hand felt at his coat and he was rather surprised to feel his wallet and some papers. His money belt too, worn underneath his trousers and his gunbelts seemed to be still in position.

At the camp there was no attempt to tie Caleb up, although he was pushed against a large rock and ordered to stay there with the warning that if he moved he would be shot. He decided that at that moment it would be wiser not to test the accuracy of that threat. For about half an hour he was completely ignored and there did not appear to be anyone keeping guard over him and he began to wonder if he could make a break for it. He had just started seriously to weigh up the possibilities when Gill Weston arrived and ordered him to his feet.

'That was you what stopped the whippin' in West Ridge, wasn't it?' He did not wait for confirmation. 'Frank is pretty sore about that, you shot him in the shoulder.'

The identity of 'Frank' became a little clearer. 'I meant to kill him,' said Caleb.

'Yeh, guess you did at that,' smiled Weston. 'Now that's one of them things that puzzles me about you. You're a minister, leastways you say you are an' I ain't about to argue with that, but I always thought ministers was in the business of savin' men's souls, not killin' 'em.'

'I am simply doing God's work,' smiled Caleb. 'He has His hands full with more important matters so I'm simply clearin' up a few loose ends.'

Weston shook his head, the reasoning seemed beyond him, as was the cynicism in Caleb's voice. 'Still don't make sense, preachers is supposed to bury the dead, not make 'em dead an' then bury 'em. I hear tell you reckon you're a bounty hunter. Now that I can understand, although as far as I'm concerned bounty hunters are the lowest form of life there is.'

'I have been known to take advantage of the reward money on offer for a man,' said Caleb. 'I don't always kill them, sometimes the reward is only if they are delivered alive and sometimes it just happens that way.'

'I guess that makes you a bounty hunter,' said Weston. 'Now, like I was sayin', Frank got mighty upset when you spoiled his fun back in West Ridge. There ain't no man on this earth better with a bull-whip than Frank Hobbs...' The identity of 'Frank' became even clearer and Caleb was forced to smile since he remembered being told once that Hobb or Hobbs was an ancient name for the Devil. It suited Frank very well. 'He can whip the legs off a fly while it's still flyin',' continued Weston. 'Have you ever seen a man after he's been bull-whipped?'

'I have had that dubious pleasure,' admitted Caleb. 'The man died.'

'They mostly do,' grinned Weston. 'I only ever knew one man who lived an' he was fit for nothin' afterwards. He might just as well have been dead for all the use he was.'

'And what exactly are your plans for me?' asked Caleb. 'Whip me to death or leave me useless?'

Weston weighed up the choice for a few

moments before grinning and spitting on the ground. 'Whip you to death I reckon,' he said eventually. 'Leastways the folk in West Ridge'll know exactly what'll happen to them if they step out of line.'

'I take it you intend to make a public spectacle of it,' said Caleb.

Weston sighed and shook his head. 'There you go again, Reveren', usin' them big words, but I guess I knows what you mean. You mean are we goin' to whip you in front of the townsfolk? Sure, that's the general idea, wouldn't have the same effect if'n they was just told about it or saw your body after. They need to hear you scream, hear you beg for mercy an' even death.'

'The name Hobbs suits Frank very well,' mused Caleb.

Weston looked at his prisoner questioningly. 'What you mean by that?'

Caleb smiled thinly and shook his head. 'A private joke,' he said. 'I don't think you'd understand.'

'Try me!' Weston suddenly ordered, thrusting his face close to Caleb's.

Caleb turned his face away from the foul

breath. 'Hobb or Hobbs is an ancient name for a goblin or even the Devil.'

Weston continued to stare at Caleb for a few moments as if digesting some wonderful new revelation. Slowly a smile spread across his face and he turned to look at Frank Hobbs. 'Hey, Frank, you hear that? The preacher here reckons that your name means...' He turned to Caleb. 'What was that other name?'

'Goblin,' replied Caleb.

'Goblin, yeh, that's right.' He turned to Frank again. 'He reckons your name means you is a goblin or the devil. How about that! Frank the Devil.'

Frank Hobbs smiled thinly. 'I already knew that, some damn fool preacher told me the same thing a long time ago.'

Weston looked a little sour as if he had just been deprived of something. 'He did? You ain't never said nothin'.' Frank simply shrugged. 'Anyhow, what's this goblin thing?' he asked Caleb.

'Some kind of evil fairy,' said Caleb.

Weston suddenly burst out laughing. 'Hell, Frank sure is evil, there ain't no gettin' away from that, but he sure ain't no fairy!' Everyone else, including Frank joined in the laughter.

'You'll find out pretty soon that I can make this whip as gentle as any fairy or as painful as anythin' the Devil could think of,' grinned Frank. He uncoiled the whip and suddenly sent it snaking towards Caleb.

Caleb did not have time to react, which was perhaps as well since the crack of the whip accompanied the removal of a button from his shirt. He did not feel any immediate pain, but was aware of a slight trickle of blood running down his chest. The pain developed a few seconds later.

'Pretty fancy,' nodded Caleb.

'You'd better believe it!' laughed Frank. 'Maybe it's lucky for you you shot me in the left shoulder, I ain't nearly so good with my other hand.'

'OK, Frank,' said Weston, 'you made your point.' He looked up at what sky was visible through the tree cover. 'I guess it's too late now, we'll go into town in the mornin'. In the meantime make the most of your last night on earth, Reveren'. Make whatever peace you got to make with your God 'cos tomorrow you'll more'n like be meetin' Him in person. Mind you, it could be that you might end up at the other place, so maybe you'd better make peace with him as well.'

Caleb was left very much to his own devices for the remaining hour of daylight, although this time there was a guard. He spent the time weighing up the surrounding landscape, what he could see of it, and gradually eliciting information from his guard.

It appeared that West Ridge was only about five miles away, which seemed to indicate that Caleb had been correct when he had thought he had gone round in circles. The lumberjack camp was also about five miles, although in a different direction, which in turn was about five miles from West Ridge.

The distances did not sound much, but from recent experience Caleb knew that five miles through thick forest, especially when one had no sense of direction, was a very long way. He made a mental note of the general direction the town lay and looked for possible landmarks, but there were none other than a high peak on the opposite side of the river which appeared to be in the exact opposite direction of West Ridge. If he could keep that peak in view behind him, he should have little difficulty. However, at that moment escape seemed impossible.

If Caleb had had any hopes that he would be left untied for the night they were quickly shattered when Weston ordered that the prisoner be bound. Caleb did protest at apparently being left where he was, claiming that he could freeze to death during the night.

'Better hope you do,' laughed Weston. 'I guess even freezin' to death is better'n Frank's bull-whip!' Caleb was inclined to agree that it might just be preferable.

The man who tied him up did a pretty good job, but he failed to notice the sharp piece of flint secreted in Caleb's hand. Gill Weston checked the bonds and seemed quite satisfied and the guard was withdrawn and for another hour the men talked noisily around the fire, during which time Caleb began working on the rope that bound his hands.

Cutting the rope was anything but easy and he even dropped his sharp flint a few times although he managed to find it again. The process was slow and even painful and, after what seemed like several hours, there appeared to be hardly any impression on the rope. Eventually he gave up the idea of trying to free his hands and to concentrate on freeing his ankles.

At first he tried to cut the ropes from behind, but quickly decided that it would be far easier if his hands were not behind his back. It took him about half an hour to work his arms along his legs and down to his feet, but eventually he was stretching himself with relief as his hands slipped under his feet.

Suddenly he was aware of someone moving and saw a shadowy figure leave the camp only to return a few moments later adjusting his trousers. Caleb feigned sleep and curled up as the man came towards him and hoped that he would not notice that Caleb's hands were no longer behind his back. The man paused for a moment, grunted slightly and returned to his bed, apparently unaware of what had happened. Caleb did not move for some time in order to allow the man time to get to sleep.

Eventually, when he was quite certain everyone was asleep, Caleb sat up and began working on the rope around his ankles. This time it was much easier, although the flint seemed to have lost most of its sharpness and took quite a considerable time to cut through. Suddenly the rope eased and Caleb quickly pulled it away, although a second knot meant that he had to hack at the rope again, since he had found it impossible to use his fingers to untie the knots.

He had only just released his ankles when another man stood up and wandered off and when he returned Caleb once again feigned sleep after roughly winding the rope around his ankles. This time the man hardly gave him a glance, although once again Caleb had to curb his activities until he was quite certain that everyone was asleep again.

Caleb was quite convinced that it was almost dawn as he eventually stood up and looked about. What sky he could see seemed distinctly lighter than earlier.

A quick glance at the men on the ground around the now dead embers of the fire seemed to indicate that they were still asleep. For a brief moment he was very tempted to take one of their guns, although with his hands still tied he thought that it might well be more of a hindrance than a help. At that moment a knife would have been far more useful and appropriate but such a thing was not to be seen and he did not intend to waste his time looking for one.

Very quietly, Caleb circled the sleeping men until he was heading off in the general direction of West Ridge. At least he hoped that was the case as in the dark even previously obvious directions seemed to take on a new confusion.

The one thing that Caleb was very

surprised at was just how difficult it was for him to make good headway. This time the problem was not the trees or the darkness or the hidden hazards, it was, surprisingly, the fact that his hands were tied. Inevitably he tripped several times making, or so it seemed at the time, enough noise to even waken the folk in West Ridge.

Each time he fell, he found it difficult to stand up again and it made him realize just how reliant on his hands he was. As he progressed he knew that he had been right about one thing, the lighter sky had been the heralder of the dawn and eventually even the gloom of the forest became clearer although it was still almost impossible to see underfoot in a great many places.

He had been blundering his way for what seemed like an hour and, as far as he could tell, he was no nearer West Ridge. His idea of using the high peak directly behind him as a guide had proved useless in the dark and he had deliberately chosen not to follow the trail back to West Ridge for fear that had his disappearance been discovered early, some of them would have used the trail. Eventually he felt that he really did need to rest and, more importantly, to untie his hands. A narrow stream and series of jagged rocks in the middle of it seemed to offer him the best chance.

SEVEN

Cutting through the rope took longer than Caleb had imagined it would and the splashing water soaked into it and had the effect of making it even tighter. Eventually though, he sighed with relief as the bonds suddenly gave way and a few minutes later he was free.

He had not realized just how tight the rope had been but as soon as the pressure was released he felt the blood painfully course back into his hands. He rubbed both wrists and hands for some time before looking around in an attempt to gain his bearings. It did not take him long to realize that he had absolutely no idea where he was or even which direction was which. What bit of sky he could see through the tree canopy was no help at all.

However, he knew that he had left the outlaw camp with the trail to West

Ridge on his left and he was reasonably certain that he had kept to a more-or-less straight course through the forest which, if correct, would mean that the trail was still somewhere to his left. Another thing that was absolutely certain was that his disappearance had been discovered some time ago.

The logical thing for him to do was find the trail and head for West Ridge and hope that he was not seen. He also had to hope that the citizens of West Ridge would rally to his defence, although he had serious doubts about that. That was the logical thing to do and as such would be expected by Gill Weston. However, he also knew that he could not simply remain hiding in the forest, even if he was able to avoid the outlaws.

The next most logical thing to do was to get as far away from West Ridge and its problems with the outlaws as he could and he silently cursed himself for becoming involved in the first place. On the other hand he knew that he could never have simply stood by and watched the bull-whipping of innocent people. He sighed heavily and resigned himself to the fact that, like it or not, he was now deeply involved and had to see it through to whatever conclusion fate threw up.

His next move was forced upon him as he suddenly became aware of the sound of someone or something coming through the undergrowth towards him. He was in no position to stand his ground and face out whoever or whatever it was, having no guns. That meant that the only thing he could do was to find somewhere to hide until the danger passed and, looking about, that did not appear to be an easy thing to do.

There were certainly no rocks large enough to hide behind, no bushes thick enough in which to conceal himself and no small caves or hollows. His glance went up to the sky again and he smiled. If there was nowhere at ground level, that only left going upwards. A nearby stout oak tree seemed to provide the answer.

The figure stopped alongside the stream at

almost the exact spot Caleb had recently been standing, looked about for a moment and suddenly grunted, bending down to pick up the remains of the rope Caleb had freed himself from. He gave them a cursory glance, grunted and looked about again.

Suddenly there were the sounds of someone else coming towards the spot, after a couple of minutes, during which time the first man simply stood his ground. The new arrival seemed more than surprised to see the first man and momentarily raised his rifle only to lower it when he realized it was not Caleb.

'Bit far out of your usual territory ain't you?' the second man said to the first.

'Just a spot of huntin',' replied the first man.

The second man laughed and swung his rifle across his shoulder. 'A spot of preacher huntin'?' he suggested.

'Preacher huntin'?' asked Sheriff Matt Brent. 'Why the hell should I be doin' somethin' like that? I'd've thought you'd've caught him by now, we sure ain't seen no sign of him in West Ridge.'

The outlaw grinned. 'Now that's somethin' of a sore point with Gill right now,' he said. 'We had him sure enough, right up till near dawn this mornin', but then it seemed he didn't like our company no more an' decided to take a walk.'

Matt Brent laughed. 'He escaped you mean! I'll say this for the guy, preacher or not, black or not, he seems kinda resourceful.'

'Don't even know what that means,' grunted the outlaw, 'but I guess you mean he can look after himself. Sure, I'll give him that. Not only that but he didn't seem too scared of Weston.'

'And such a thing impresses you?'

'Sure,' admitted the outlaw, 'any man what ain't scared of Weston has to be admired, but that don't mean I wouldn't kill the bastard if I met him.'

'Are you scared of Weston?' asked the sheriff.

The man grinned broadly. 'Let's just say I do what he tells me, it's safer that way.'

The sheriff smiled and nodded, he knew exactly what the man meant since it reflected his own feelings precisely. 'So, you lost him. If the man has any sense at all he'd be well away from here by now.'

The figure crouched in the fork of some branches high above the two men's heads silently nodded in total agreement with this observation.

'Just what I said to Weston,' said the outlaw. 'Gill, I said, if that preacher got a lick o' sense up his arse, he's crossed the river an' is high-tailin' it north an' if he has crossed the river then we might just as well forget all about him. Gill didn't seem too sure about that though an', like he pointed out, the tracks led this way, away from the river. Anyhow, he seems to think that the preacher is still hangin' around. He reckons he's got somethin' to prove. Mind you, what the hell that is or who to he ain't too sure.'

'Damned preacher!' said the sheriff, spitting into the water. 'I didn't like things the way they were, but at least we didn't have no trouble. Anyhow, I ain't seen him an' I been out since before dawn.'

The outlaw grinned and began to move away. 'You'd be doin' yourself an' us a favour if you kill him if you do come across him. He ain't got no guns as far as we know, his own are still back at the camp.'

'Maybe I'll do just that,' grunted the sheriff. He looked about and sighed heavily. 'I was hopin' to bag me a big stag I seen around here, but I guess that with all this row that's been goin' on he's miles away by now. I'll have to leave it till some other time.'

'Try some preacher huntin'!' laughed the departing outlaw.

Sheriff Matt Brent made no move for at least ten minutes, all the time appearing to be listening and looking. More than once his glance rested on the large oak tree and the remains of the rope played constantly in his fingers. Eventually he moved away from the water and leaned against the oak tree where he lit himself a cheroot and continued to play with the rope. Suddenly, without looking up, he spoke.

'Reckon you can outrun 'em, Reverend?' he asked.

Actually Caleb was rather thrown by this and was not at all certain if the sheriff was addressing him directly or simply talking aloud to himself.

'I said do you think you can outrun 'em?' repeated the sheriff, only this time a little louder.

This time Caleb knew that he was being asked a direct question.

'I done pretty well so far,' he heard himself responding.

The sheriff certainly showed no surprise at hearing the voice. 'So far,' he agreed, 'but even you can't stay lucky for ever.'

There seemed little point in remaining up the tree and Caleb struggled down to the ground. It had seemed easy enough to climb up, but then he had had a definite interest in gaining height. Eventually he was on the ground and dusting himself off.

'How'd you know I was up there?'

'Didn't,' shrugged the sheriff. 'Just an educated guess.' He held up the rope. 'I guessed that they would have caught you, 'specially since they told me at the lumberjack camp you'd headed for the outlaw camp an' not returned.'

'OK,' grinned Caleb. 'Right on every count so far. Why didn't you just tell that outlaw where you thought I was?'

'Probably 'cos I never figured it out until after he'd gone,' he admitted. 'Mind, I ain't so sure as I would've said anythin' even if I had worked it out.'

'So what now?'

'So nothin' now,' shrugged Matt. 'Least-ways as far as I'm concerned. Just one thing, I got to thank you for what you did back in West Ridge, you know, savin' them two boys.'

'Boys?' queried Caleb.

'Well, as far as I'm concerned they're still boys,' smiled the sheriff. 'One of 'em is my son.'

'Your son!' exclaimed Caleb. 'Do you mean you were prepared to just stand by and watch your own flesh and blood be whipped to death? I don't understand you at all!'

'That whip would never have reached either of them,' assured Matt. 'Mind, I'd more'n like be dead by now an' just maybe they'd've whipped 'em anyhow, so it would've been a waste of time.'

Caleb raised his hand to his mouth to hide his embarrassment. 'I'm sorry, Sheriff, I didn't realize you were prepared to kill them.'

'Why should you?' said Matt. 'It ain't no concern of yours, leastways it wasn't until you shot Frank Hobbs.'

'Yeh,' agreed Caleb. 'I guess that did make it my business.'

'You must've heard what Jake said, about crossin' the river an' they'd never be able to find you. He's right, it's pretty damned wild up there but the worst thing you got to watch out for is bears an' wolves. Wolves don't normally bother a man but some of them damned bears can be mighty dangerous.'

Caleb laughed loudly, suddenly clamping his hand across his mouth to shut himself

151

up. He looked about and listened but could hear nothing. 'No need to tell me about bears,' he said, almost whispering. 'I had a run in with one yesterday. That's how come I got caught. If it hadn't been for that damned bear I think I'd never have been caught.'

'Yeh, we still get the odd one this side of the river from time to time,' said Matt. 'Apart from the one they call Ben at the lumberjack camp, they ain't been too common since they started fellin' timber.'

'I heard this Jake, or whatever he's called, say that Weston thought I had somethin' to prove. I don't know about having to prove anything, but he's right in a way. I feel I've started something which I am duty bound to see the end of.'

'Or get yourself killed in the attempt which don't do nobody no good at all,' said Matt. 'Ever thought it might just be better to forget all about it an' leave well alone?'

'Briefly,' admitted Caleb. 'Is that what you think?'

'If you'd asked me that when you first came into town an' suggested takin' Coyne an' Gates, I'd've been very definite about it, leave things be. The trouble is it's gone past that now an' the way things are they're headin' for a showdown with Weston.'

'It wasn't me who made the first move,' reminded Caleb.

'That's what makes it worse,' grunted the sheriff. 'Anyhow, I don't know what your next move is goin' to be, but I wouldn't show my face in town just yet if I was you. As things stand right now most of 'em is for handin' you over to Weston.'

'Thanks for the warning,' said Caleb. 'I had thought about going there.'

'I won't ask just what you intend doin',' said Matt. 'That's one of them things I think I'm better off not knowin'.' He looked at Caleb's crossed gun belts and at the empty holsters. 'I ain't got two guns,' he said at length, taking his own Colt from its holster and offering it, handle first, to Caleb, 'but you'd better take this, you might just need it.'

Caleb was more than surprised by this

action. Guns were very expensive items of hardware and he had never known anyone give one away willingly. However, whether because he *was* surprised or because he agreed that he really needed a gun, he took it, briefly tested the weight in his hand and seemed satisfied and slipped it into the holster on his right hip.

'Thanks, Sheriff,' he said, with genuine admiration for a man he had previously had more than a little contempt for. 'I won't ask why, let's just say I'm grateful.'

The sheriff looked a little uncomfortable and stared at the ground. 'Well, I came out here to shoot a big stag, maybe I should start lookin' for him.'

'I think you were right when you said he probably won't be around here now, not with all the noise,' reminded Caleb. 'Me, I need to hole up somewhere a while and think things over.'

'Follow this creek downstream for about a mile,' suggested Matt. 'You'll find some old mine workin's. There's so many tunnels a man could hide out forever there an' not get caught.'

'I might just do that,' agreed Caleb. He turned and began to follow the stream, not waiting to see where the sheriff went or what he did. He now felt more reassured by the weight of the gun in the holster, especially since the outlaws seemed convinced that he was unarmed.

The mines would have been easy to miss had he not been looking for them. It was plain that they had not been used for a good many years, now overgrown with thick bushes and even small trees which had managed to take root in seemingly the most impossible of positions.

However, as inexperienced in woodsmanship as he was, even Caleb could not miss the obvious signs that someone or something had been here very recently and he could not be certain that they were still not in the area. So, to be on the safe side, he settled himself between two large rocks and waited and while he waited his thoughts turned inevitably to what he was going to do next.

For once, his caution proved correct; about half an hour after he had settled down, he heard a rather ghostly voice as it echoed from a nearby mine entrance to be followed a short time later by another, less distinct voice apparently from deeper in the mine. After about five minutes the figure of Seth, the outlaw who had taken possession of his rifle appeared, coughed loudly and spat foully on to the ground, wheezed and rummaged in his jacket pocket. He produced a rather battered looking cheroot which he carefully straightened and repaired before striking a match on a nearby rock and lighting it. As the smoke coursed into his chest he once again coughed, choked and spluttered.

Caleb was no more than five yards from the man and it would have been very easy to shoot him and recover his rifle and for a brief moment that was exactly what he was tempted to do but just in time he remembered the other voice. It was about two minutes later that the other outlaw emerged into the daylight.

'Waste of time if you ask me,' grumbled

Seth. 'Ain't no reason why he should've come this way; he's a stranger, he don't know 'bout this place.'

'He could've found it by accident,' reasoned the second man. 'Still, we've been through most of it an' there ain't no sign of him nor anyone else. I'm for forgettin' about the rest, Gill ain't goin' to know we never looked.'

'I'm for that,' agreed Seth. 'Better hang on here a while though, he'd know if we got back too soon.'

Both men moved away from the entrance and sat on a rock, Seth coughing and choking as he inhaled the smoke from his cheroot. In moving they had placed themselves closer to where Caleb was hidden and, more importantly, they now had their backs towards him.

Stealth was another thing that Caleb was very inexperienced in, mainly because he had never had to be. Normally he was faced with a 'him-or-me' situation which, until now had always turned out to be 'me' coming out on top.

Caleb was now faced with the choice of

shooting the men, even though it meant shooting them in the back, and creeping up on them and using his newly acquired gun to knock them out. Shooting them in the back presented no qualms, he had done so before when it had been necessary and would do so again. This time however, he was loath to do so since he could not be certain that other men were not in the area and would be attracted by the shooting, something he did not want at that moment.

There was just one problem about creeping up on the men: it meant negotiating a large, slippery looking rock and a small but very thick bush. He thought about the alternatives for a moment and decided that he really did not have any option, he had to shoot.

'What the hell are you doin' here?' demanded Seth, leaping to his feet and raising his rifle. 'Stupid bastard, you could've got yourself killed.'

'Would that have bothered you?' asked the new arrival.

Caleb sank back between his rocks, silently cursing.

'Not 'specially,' admitted Seth. 'Didn't know you was workin' this part.'

'I work anywhere,' grunted The Beast. 'I been told to find a particular size tree, somethin' to do with a special order. Got to be a certain thickness.'

'Found it?' asked the other outlaw.

'I reckon I found what I was lookin' for,' smiled The Beast, casually swinging his gleaming axe on to his shoulder. 'You found what you're lookin' for?'

'Who says we're lookin' for anythin'?' said Seth, defensively.

'The fact you're here,' grinned The Beast. 'Let me guess, you're lookin' for that preacher guy.'

'Could be,' nodded Seth. 'You ain't seen him have you?'

The big man grinned broadly. 'Sure, I seen him; in fact I'm lookin' at him right now, he's right behind you!'

Caleb's stomach leapt into his mouth, the two men spun round and suddenly the axe slung across The Beast's shoulder swung and landed with a dull, sickening thud into the neck of the second outlaw and, before Seth had time to realize just what was happening, the axe swung again...

'My God!' gasped Caleb, coming from his hiding place and gazing down at the grisly scene.

Seth's head had been split down the middle and the other man's head was almost completely severed. Caleb was not normally affected by gory sights, but this one had the effect of making his stomach lurch and he had difficulty keeping the contents of it inside him. Blood still pumped from the gaping wound of the unknown outlaw but, very surprisingly as far as Caleb was concerned, there was relatively little blood coming from the divided head of Seth.

The Beast seemed totally unaffected either by what he had done or the scene. He smiled at Caleb and proceeded to wipe the bloody blade of his axe on Seth's clothes.

'Figured you might need some help,' said The Beast, casually. 'I met Sheriff

Brent an' he told me he'd sent you this way. I'd not long come from here an' I'd seen these two searchin' the mines.'

Caleb wiped his strangely dry mouth on his sleeve and licked his lips. 'Thanks,' he said, 'I was just about to shoot them myself.'

'My way's the best,' grinned The Beast, 'gunshots tend to attract attention. This way nobody is ever goin' to know.'

'Not until they find the bodies,' said Caleb still staring at the mutilated corpses in a hypnotic fascination.

The Beast laughed, laid down his axe—much to Caleb's relief since he had visions of the huge blade slicing through his head—picked up Seth's feet and indicated that Caleb do the same with the other outlaw. Without another word The Beast dragged the body inside the mine about twenty yards. Caleb did the same, but took care to remove the guns from each body, which now meant that he had three hand-guns and two rifles.

Caleb still considered that it would not take Gill Weston long to discover the bodies, although it really did not matter that much if he did except that now, because of the type of injuries, the loggers would be clearly implicated. Apparently though, this did not concern The Beast at all and Caleb soon discovered why.

The Beast told Caleb to leave the mine ahead of him and he had no sooner cleared the entrance than The Beast began swinging his axe at the rotted wooden pit props. At first there was little more than a few creaks and groans and a faint trickle of dry dust from the roof but, after about two minutes there was a crash of rock followed by dust and grit billowing out of the shaft, making Caleb choke and cough as he was forced to back away.

Eventually the dust settled and Caleb peered into the entrance to find that it was now totally blocked. He smiled slightly, knowing that there was now no chance of Gill Weston ever discovering exactly what had happened to his men. That they were under the rockfall would be fairly obvious, but it was very doubtful if anyone would bother to look.

Afterwards, he and The Beast sat on the same rock the outlaws had been sitting on, Caleb aware of a dark stain on the ground by his feet which even now was attracting ants and other insects. It would not be long before nature destroyed even this evidence.

'Remind me not to get on the wrong end of that axe of yours,' said Caleb. 'I don't reckon I could have shot them any quicker.'

'Yeh,' replied The Beast, rather proudly, 'I am pretty good ain't I? It's been a long time since I did somethin' like that.'

Caleb found that he was not at all surprised at this apparent admission that the big man had done such a thing before. He had only ever come across lumberjacks briefly before and had never even spoken to any of them, but they had struck him at that time as a breed all of their own and not to be trifled with.

'Did you really know I was there?' asked Caleb.

'Sure,' grinned The Beast. 'It's plain you ain't never been used to the forest. I was lookin' down on you just before they came out of the mine.' Caleb looked up at a large, flat rock and nodded slightly. 'I heard one of 'em call, just like you did, so I circled round and bided my time.'

'Once again, I thank you,' said Caleb. 'But I am somewhat puzzled as to why you should bother.'

'Me too, come to think of it,' admitted The Beast. 'I guess it's just that life's been a bit dull hereabouts lately'

Caleb decided that that explanation was the only one he was likely to get and did not pursue the matter. Since he now had more guns than he needed, he somehow felt obliged to offer the extra hand gun and rifle to the big man. The Beast took both, rested the pistol in his huge hand and laughed. Caleb too had to laugh; in The Beast's huge fist the gun looked like some puny toy and it was obvious that those huge hands would not be able to handle the weapon properly. The Big man laughed and tossed the gun back to Caleb but he examined the rifle with interest.

'Now this I can make use of,' he said. 'I

used to have me a rifle once, big old thing it was, what they call a buffalo gun, but it sort of just broke.'

Now Caleb could well appreciate a man of The Beast's stature behind a muzzle loading buffalo gun. These were huge, heavy, long-barrelled guns which needed a rest for the barrel, but their fire power was truly awesome, which was why they were used for hunting buffalo, being just about the only gun guaranteed to stop a charging animal in its tracks.

'So now what do you do?' asked The Beast. 'If you got any sense at all you'll get the hell out of it. I can feel trouble brewin' between Weston an' the town.'

'And since I started the trouble, I think I ought to be there to end it,' said Caleb.

The Beast looked at the preacher quizzically for a moment. 'Naw, you didn't start no trouble, that was there long before you turned up. All you did was bring matters to a head a bit quicker'n might have happened.'

'I still feel I ought to be there,' insisted Caleb.

The big man shrugged. 'That's your business. Me an' the boys? We ain't really decided what we're goin' to do. Townsfolk don't like us that much so why should we bother?'

'Indeed, why should you?' agreed Caleb with a certain amount of sincerity.

EIGHT

'Rock fall,' announced the outlaw, Frank Hobbs, as he and Gill Weston examined the entrance to the mine. 'I'd lay my last dollar on the two of 'em bein' somewhere underneath.'

'They could be trapped inside,' suggested Weston, not really convinced by his own argument. 'I did hear of a miner bein' trapped for two weeks 'fore they got him out.'

'Maybe so,' Hobbs agreed somewhat grudgingly, 'but you can see for yourself can't you an' we have tried callin' both here an' in that other shaft. Naw, I'd say they was dead all right an' with a bit of luck that damned preacher is in there with 'em.'

'I sure hope not,' grunted Weston. 'I want that feller alive just so's I can see the hell beaten out of him.'

'Well I hope he's dead,' responded Hobbs. 'Sure, I would've enjoyed whippin' the hide off him, but it seems to me that he's caused nothin' but trouble ever since he showed up.'

Gill Weston pulled away a loose rock in the pile and both men suddenly jumped back in alarm as other rocks above moved ominously They decided that the safest place to be was outside.

'You is right about him bein' a load of trouble,' said Weston, peering into the gloom, 'but I still want him alive but maybe it's better if he is dead. Still, right now we've got to work on the basis that he ain't dead an' that he's out there somewhere. You're the one with the schoolin', if that was you on the run out there, where would you go?'

'North, across the river,' said Hobbs firmly. 'Anyone with a lick o' sense would know we wouldn't stand no chance of catchin' him up there.'

'Me too,' agreed Weston. 'Thing is, I got me this feelin' that he knows that but he ain't about to do what's obvious. I think he's out to prove somethin'.'

Frank Hobbs laughed. 'Have you ever met any man what gives a damn about what happens to other folk or who hangs about just tryin' to prove he can beat another man?' Weston shook his head. 'Then why the hell should a black preacher be any different?'

'Dunno,' agreed Weston, 'but then I ain't never met a black preacher before, leastways not one what carries two guns an' makes a livin' bounty huntin'.'

Hobbs laughed again. 'Talk!' he declared. 'All talk! Preachers is good at talkin', that's why they is preachers. It's his job to convince folk what don't believe that there is a God up there somewhere. Thing is they ain't never once been able to produce any proof, 'ceptin' words an' I reckon he's the same when it comes to bounty huntin'. I ain't sayin' he don't pick up the odd outlaw from time to time, even you an' me could do that.'

'What about the two guns?' asked Weston.

Frank Hobbs had no real answer to

that and simply shook his head before walking away.

'You comin',' he asked Weston, 'or are you goin' to try an' move them rocks all on your own?'

Gill Weston sighed, realizing that to attempt to move the blockage would probably prove nothing and would certainly take far too long to accomplish. He had to accept that his two missing men were probably lying crushed beneath the fall and there was the possibility that the preacher, Caleb Black was also buried, although he had the uneasy feeling that he was not.

'West Ridge,' announced Weston. 'We go into West Ridge. Everythin' centres on the town, he ain't got no other reason for hangin' about. If he ain't showed up there already, it's just a matter of time 'fore he does.'

'That makes sense,' agreed Hobbs. 'Only thing is, if he ain't there yet, he sure ain't likely to show up if he knows we're there.'

Gill Weston grinned broadly. 'Then we'll just have to make him show up!'

Caleb had thought of making his way to West Ridge but then he started to think that was what Weston would expect him to do and ruled the idea out for the moment at least. If his calculations were correct, Gill Weston was now left with four men plus himself, although even after having spent the best part of a day and night in their camp he still could not be absolutely certain of the number.

However, whether there had been seven of them or even ten of them before, the simple fact was that there were now two less, although even with five remaining it was four more than he would care to have to face unless it was absolutely unavoidable.

The Beast had suggested that he, Caleb, return to the loggers' camp with him but Caleb had turned down the offer. Although he had been very tempted to accept and he felt that all except one could be trusted, it was the presence of the odd one which deterred him.

The odd man out was, of course, Cripple

Dyke, the man now confined to cooking and cleaning for the lumberjacks. He had managed to extort money out of Caleb before and, although he would not be able to do so again, Caleb had the feeling that Cripple Dyke would be only too willing to inform Gill Weston where he was—for a price, of course.

So, faced with the fact that the logging camp was out and that it was probably unsafe to go into West Ridge for the moment, Caleb's problem was where to hide himself and also to know when it would be right for him to make his next move. He smiled to himself as he considered the one possibility that even Gill Weston might not consider—he would return to the outlaw camp; at least he would place himself in a position to see and possibly hear what was happening. There was, of course, another good reason for returning to the camp, he would need a horse and that was where his was. He would have also liked to have his own guns, but he was not too worried if that proved impossible.

The Beast had, in a few short sentences, given Caleb some idea how to judge which way he was facing in the forest, although he was uncertain if he would ever be able to put them into practice. The hint about moss growing only on the north-facing side of rocks and trees seemed to become meaningless the first time he tried it.

After walking around a large boulder several times, Caleb was forced to the conclusion that all faces of the boulder pointed north, although the moss did seem thicker on one side than the others, so he took that direction to be north.

Whether by chance or due to the fact that he had read the message of the moss correctly, Caleb was very surprised when he suddenly found himself overlooking the outlaw camp, a camp which at first appeared deserted.

Gill Weston had insisted on riding back via the lumberjacks' camp purely on the off-chance that their quarry had taken refuge there. While he knew that he would get no help or information from most of them, there was one who could be relied upon. As expected the arrival of the two outlaws in the loggers' camp was obviously not well received.

The outlaws' questions were met with non committal grunts or a deaf ear and both men sensed a distinct animosity towards them and decided that their safety was very much in question and left. However, before they left, the one man whom they could trust in any way drew Gill Weston to one side.

'Where'd you get that rifle?' Weston asked The Beast, rather nervously. 'It looks like the one Slim used to own.'

'Well he don't now,' grinned The Beast as if challenging either of them to take the rifle from him.

'I ain't arguin' that,' said Weston, resting his hand on the gun slung at his hip partly in an attempt to threaten The Beast and partly to reassure himself. 'I know it's his though, there's a piece missin' out of the stock.'

The Beast looked at the stock and

laughed. 'Well, so it has. What you goin' to do about it?'

Both outlaws glanced nervously at each other and then at the other loggers seemingly standing or sitting idly around but all either stroking rifles or pointedly running their fingers along very sharp axe blades. It was the sight and thought of the axe blades which decided them.

'Nothin',' croaked Weston. 'Just curious. Slim an' Seth are both missin'.'

The Beast grinned. 'Guess that explains it then. There was a cave-in in the old mines, I found the rifle there.'

Neither Weston nor Hobbs had the nerve to ask any further questions and The Beast did seem to confirm what they thought and they both hastily left the camp. As the outlaws left, The Beast closed in on Cripple Dyke...

Caleb had not really considered time; in many respects it did not seem that long since he had first escaped the camp but a glance at the sun through the relatively unrestricted view from the outlaw camp seemed to indicate that it was in fact a lot later than he imagined. A glance at the pocket watch he normally ensured was as accurate as possible showed that it had stopped. He cursed himself for the oversight of not winding it, but consoled himself that this was due to being otherwise occupied at the time.

Even so and with Caleb's somewhat limited ability to read the position of the sun with any accuracy, he judged that it must be within a couple of hours of sunset. He found a sheltered spot overlooking the camp and waited.

He did not have to wait long before men slowly ambled back, all on foot having been searching the forest. As he had waited he had seen one man in the camp but he appeared to be alone. The arrival of the others gave Caleb the opportunity to discover exactly how many of them there were.

It appeared that the men had been searching in pairs, since that was the way they arrived back. The first two to arrive were in fact Gill Weston and

Frank Hobbs, followed five minutes later by two more arriving almost immediately below where Caleb was hiding. A third pair arrived about half an hour later and these seemed to be the last. Caleb was now reasonably certain that he was facing seven men.

Odd words floated upwards but Caleb was unable to make sense of anything that was said, although he was reasonably certain that he was the chief topic of conversation since he could make out the word 'preacher' every now and then.

What his next move was going to be, Caleb had no idea at all. He had hoped for some inspiration to strike him but such a thing was singularly absent. It would have been a relatively easy matter to shoot any one of them with his rifle, but although he seriously considered making Gill Weston his main target, he knew that one shot was all the chance he would have. Although at that distance there was little doubt that his bullet would strike its target, there was always some doubt as to just how accurate the shot would be, even an inch either way could mean the difference between killing and maiming.

Not only would he only get the one chance to kill Weston, his position would be exposed at once which would mean him taking to the forest once again and he did not relish the idea of stumbling through that lot again in the dark. He decided to bide his time until the morning.

Caleb awoke with a start. There was the vague hint of light in the sky heralding the new day, but it was not an hour that he was used to seeing too often.

However, it had not been the first hint of daylight which had woken him, it had been the unmistakable sound of horses galloping but, peer into the gloom as much as he could, Caleb could not make out a thing.

This annoyed him slightly, but he knew that all he could do was wait until it was light enough to see and then make his plans—if he had any ideas at all.

It was probably no more than a few minutes before the sky had lightened sufficiently to see fairly clearly but it felt a very long time. Eventually though, Caleb was looking down on to what appeared to be a deserted camp and some of the horses were definitely missing. However, whilst Caleb may have lacked experience in woodsmanship or tracking, caution was something that he had in abundance, sometimes too much he thought.

This time his caution paid off yet again as a man suddenly appeared, obviously having just woken up as he yawned and scratched himself thoroughly. This action had the effect of making Caleb feel quite itchy and he could not resist the urge to scratch himself and briefly examine his own chest for fleas and ticks. He thought he saw a flea but he lost it and the urge to scratch increased but he resisted.

The man appeared to be alone, although Caleb did wait another ten minutes before deciding on his next move and when it came it was not so much of a conscious decision as an automatic reaction. He slowly descended into the outlaw camp.

It was quite obvious that the man

apparently left on guard was not expecting anyone least of all Caleb. The look on his face when he was suddenly faced by Caleb and a gun aimed steadily at him was one of sheer horror and he offered no resistance at all as he was disarmed.

'Where have they gone?' Caleb demanded as he proceeded to tie the man to the base of a nearby tree. He was taking no chances, he did not want anyone roaming around.

The man now seemed more relaxed as if somehow secure in the knowledge that he was not about to be killed. 'West Ridge,' he said. 'Although what good that's goin' to do you I don't know.'

'I just like to know where the opposition is,' said Caleb, checking the rope. 'What have they gone there for?'

'If you hang about long enough you'll find out,' grunted the outlaw. 'I hear Frank is bitin' on the bit, somethin' about wantin' to finish off a job you interrupted.'

'Whipping!' said Caleb. 'What good will that do?'

The man tried to shrug but found it difficult. 'I reckon it's 'cos he enjoys it.'

'Is that all?' urged Caleb.

'All I know to,' said the outlaw. 'I'd say you've seen enough of Frank to know what he's like. He's what they call a sadist or somethin'.'

'I'd say that was a fair description,' agreed Caleb. 'I still don't see the point of it though.'

The man laughed. 'Frank Hobbs don't need no excuse, but Gill's got some idea 'bout forcin' you out of the forest on account of he reckons you won't just stand by an' watch folk bein' whipped.'

'I am rapidly coming to the conclusion that I really don't give a damn,' grunted Caleb.

'That ain't the way it looks from where I'm sittin',' grinned the outlaw. 'If that is the case, why the hell ain't you miles away from here?'

'Why indeed?' mused Caleb. 'The thing is you've got my horse. I need a horse if I'm to get away.'

The man nodded in the general direction of the remaining horses. 'Over there, saddles too. Now's your chance.'

'You're being very helpful,' said Caleb. 'Don't you want to see me dead?'

'Reveren',' sighed the man, 'I couldn't care less what happens to you. If need be I'll be the one to kill you, but I sure won't lose no sleep about it if you decide to get the hell out of it. I know that's what I'd do if I was in your position.'

'There's no doubt about it,' said Caleb, 'what you say is the logical thing to do. With me out of the way Weston would have no cause to inflict any punishment on anyone and things could get back to just how they were.'

'Now you're talkin' sense,' grinned the man. 'Untie me an' I'll even help you saddle up.'

Caleb grinned and shook his head. 'In the Lord I trust,' he said, 'but my fellow men I treat with care in such matters. If you don't mind—or even if you do—I'll leave you tied here. Another thing, you took my guns off me. I know I've got two more, but a man gets used to the feel and weight of his own. Where are they?'

'Ain't sure,' admitted the outlaw, 'but

if they're anywhere they're probably with your saddle.'

Caleb grunted, checked that the man was securely bound and then went to where the horses were. His own horse was still there and, rather surprisingly, he did find his own guns alongside his saddle. He handled them fondly for a moment before exchanging them for the two in his belts, which he then slid into one of his saddle-bags. Also, again rather surprisingly, he discovered that the contents of his saddle bags had not been disturbed and three boxes of ammunition were still intact.

He saddled his horse and led her back to where the outlaw was still tied to the tree and it appeared that he had not made any attempt to escape.

'I've been thinking,' he announced to the outlaw. 'I've been thinking that it does make sense for me to get away from here. With me out of the way everyone, including the townsfolk, will be much happier. I don't know if you realize it, but even the good folk of West Ridge think I'm a pain in the arse and most of them are all for handing me over to Weston.'

'So you're runnin' out,' goaded the outlaw.

'Not running out,' said Caleb, 'making what we used to call in the army a strategic withdrawal.'

'Like I said, runnin' out!' grinned the man.

'Call it what you will,' sighed Caleb. 'Now, I do hear that if I had any sense I would cross the river and head north. Apparently there's virtually no chance of being caught up there.'

'It'd be a waste of time anyone tryin',' agreed the outlaw. 'Only things up there are wolves an' bears an' I do hear there's a few Indians who ain't too friendly towards white men. Renegades I think they're called. You know, mainly young bucks who resent the way their chiefs have given in to the white man or have been cast out of their tribes for one reason or another.'

Caleb laughed and stroked his face. 'White men? I don't know if it has struck you, but I am most definitely not white.

Do you think they feel the same way about black men?'

The outlaw cocked his head to one side and looked quizzically at Caleb for a moment. Suddenly he burst out laughing. 'Reveren', I can honestly say that that's somethin' I ain't never thought about before. It could just be that your black skin might mean you keepin' your scalp, that is if neither the wolves or the bears don't get you first. One thing I am sure of is that they don't give a damn what colour a man's skin is, to them you probably taste just the same as a white man.'

Caleb smiled. 'At least if they do eat me I shall know they don't hold any grudge on that score.' He mounted his horse and adjusted the saddle bags slightly. 'Now, the river is that way. Is there an easy way down to it?'

'Just follow your nose that way,' the outlaw indicated, nodding his head. 'It's a steep path but fairly wide. You'd best cross here, further up it gets pretty rough an' the other way is deep.'

'I thank you,' said Caleb, touching the

brim of his black hat. 'Now, I'm sorry I can't release you, but I am sure you will not have too long to wait. Thank you for being so helpful and understanding. Tell Mr Weston that I am sorry I couldn't hang about and that perhaps one day we shall meet again, although I sincerely hope not.'

'You'd better hope you don't,' said the outlaw.

Caleb smiled, touched the brim of his hat again and urged his horse forward. As the outlaw had said, the path down to the river was steep but quite safe and a few minutes later his horse was picking its way across the rocky river-bed. There was not a lot of water flowing and the main channel proved to be quite shallow and about fifteen minutes after leaving the outlaw camp, Caleb and horse were clambering up a steep, rocky face, Caleb having dismounted to lead his horse. At the top he looked back across the river to where he knew the camp to be but there was no sign of life. He sighed and smiled to himself before remounting.

'Are you sure about that?' Gill Weston demanded as the man left to guard the camp was untied.

'Sure as anyone can be,' said the man, rubbing life back into his wrists and hands. 'I didn't actually see him cross the river but I reckon that's where he went.'

Weston turned to two other men. 'Get down there an' see if you can find his tracks. I don't trust that bastard, for all I know he could be somewhere up there watchin' us right now.'

The two men hurried off down the path and Weston turned to a man sitting on a horse, a man whom Caleb, had he been there, would have recognized as the son of Sheriff Matt Brent.

'I guess that puts paid to your plans,' said the young man.

'Maybe, maybe not,' said Weston. 'I still don't trust that preacher. It don't make sense for a man to go through what he's been through an' then just give everythin' up.'

'Even if he has,' said Frank Hobbs, 'I

think we should still whip the hide off this young feller just to show the rest of the town we mean business.'

Gill Weston did not answer that observation. 'Now what would I do if I was in the preacher's shoes?' he mused. 'Sure, I'd probably do the same, pretend I was leavin', go across the river an' then double back.'

'It could be that he really has decided to run,' said one of the other men.

'Could be,' Weston agreed somewhat doubtfully. 'Only one way to find out, we proceed as if he was still around. Like Frank says, even if he ain't, it'll serve to show the folk in town that we mean business.'

This observation had the effect of making Frank Hobbs grin broadly at the young man and begin to uncoil his bull whip in anticipation. Weston shook his head and sighed.

'When?' asked Frank Hobbs.

'Not yet,' said Weston. 'If that preacher has decided to double back we've got to give him time.'

As Gill Weston had expected, the two men returned from the river with the news that there were very definite signs that Caleb had recently crossed to the northern bank.

NINE

As Caleb had looked down, he had suddenly realized that both he and his horse had scaled what appeared to be an almost sheer cliff of about 300 feet. From where he was, at the top, it looked an impossible climb but he recalled that it had not looked quite so severe from the bottom.

At that moment it would have been only too easy to take the advice he was constantly being offered and turn his back on West Ridge and head north. His own reasoning that his departure would even benefit the citizens of West Ridge in some way, even began to make sense to him. However, whether it was pure stubbornness on his part or a sort of twisted belief that the people of the town really did need his services, he had already decided that he was going to help them whether they liked it or not.

The outlaw on guard had told him that Gill Weston wanted to lure him into West Ridge and he could see no reason why he should disappoint him. As ever, any idea of just how he was going to tackle the situation did not even begin to form in his mind, he would take things as they came as usual. He had discovered from past experiences that carefully laid plans had the nasty habit of becoming meaningless.

It seemed that he was never going to find a spot where he could re-cross the river; there were many places he could have done so with ease, had he not been 300 feet above the river bed. In fact, the further downstream he went, the higher and steeper the sides seemed to be, but he put that down to an illusion as the gorge narrowed.

Eventually, after what seemed like three or four hours but he guessed that in reality was little more than an hour, he came across a steep, extremely narrow fissure which led down to the river bed. A brief examination showed that there was some sort of track, probably made by goats or deer and he decided that if they could negotiate the fissure, so could he.

About half-way down he began to wonder if he could even make it back to the top since it looked increasingly likely that he might have to retrace his steps. The walls of the fissure had closed in to the point where they almost created a tunnel and while goats and deer may have been able to pass through quite easily, a horse complete with saddle was a different matter.

However, with much pushing and cajoling, Caleb somehow managed to force his horse through what turned out to be the narrowest section. From that point on the going was comparatively easy although the further down they went the more slippery became the surface and more than once both he and horse slithered dangerously.

The river-bed was eventually reached and both Caleb and horse could not have been more winded than when they had climbed out of the valley and they rested for a while before continuing.

Being much narrower than before, the

river now cascaded over rocks and rapids and at first appeared almost impossible to cross, but Caleb noted that the track he had been following seemed to disappear into the water and a scrutiny of the opposite bank, now only about fifty feet or so away, indicated that it emerged and followed the line of a large rock sloping upwards from the river-bed.

It seemed that the goats and deer had chosen well, the short crossing was even but not slippery and the path up the rock on the other side proved fairly wide. The top was reached with comparative ease and Caleb followed another well-defined trail through a short, narrow, tree covered gorge and suddenly found himself coming out on to what was plainly the main trail between the outlaw camp and West Ridge.

This time he had no difficulty in deciding which way to go; to his left would lead him back to the outlaws and to his right into West Ridge. Although he still had unfinished business with Gill Weston, he felt that the time was not yet right for a showdown. At the same time he was uncertain as to the reception he would receive in West Ridge which, hostile as it might be, would be a whole lot safer than facing Gill Weston.

As things turned out, Caleb never reached the town. He had travelled perhaps a mile when he saw a group of men talking, one of whom was easily recognizable as The Beast. Two others proved to be the lumberjacks Lord Jim and The Piper, the fourth man, rather surprisingly, turned out to be Sheriff Matt Brent astride his horse.

At first all four men eyed Caleb's arrival with great suspicion which was heightened when they realized it was the preacher. The last thing they had expected was to see him on a horse.

'Where'd you get that?' demanded the sheriff.

'Gill Weston and his men seemed to have more horses than they needed,' grinned Caleb. 'Anyhow, it is my horse, so nobody can accuse me of horse stealing.'

'You know what I mean,' grated the sheriff. 'Gill Weston's out to kill you so he ain't about to let you just ride off.'

'He didn't know anything about it at the time,' said Caleb. 'I was just on my way into town to see you, Sheriff.'

'Then it's just as well you met me out here,' came the terse reply. 'Right now you ain't exactly very popular. You're even less welcome than you were yesterday.'

'But I haven't even been into town,' protested Caleb. 'Why should they hate me more now?'

'Two men badly injured and one taken hostage,' said the sheriff 'The doc reckons the two injured will be OK, but there's no knowin' what's goin' to happen to my boy, though we can all guess.'

'Your boy?' queried Caleb. 'The one who was going to be bull-whipped?'

'That's the one, the only boy I've got,' replied Matt Brent.

'And I take it he's the one they've taken hostage,' said Caleb.

'Right first time,' hissed Brent. 'The word is you have to be held if you show up and handed over to Weston and I can assure you, Mr Preacherman, that's exactly what folk in town intend doin'.'

'And you?' asked Caleb.

Matt Brent slumped in his saddle and looked hard at Caleb, seemingly giving the matter a great deal of thought. 'I guess I've got more reason than anyone to do what Weston says,' he said eventually, 'but if you choose to keep on ridin' I'll pretend I ain't never seen you.'

'And your boy?'

The sheriff spat angrily on to the ground and glared at Caleb again. 'When I left town I had me this crazy idea of ridin' into Weston's camp an' shootin' the place up, but I had me some time to think. For a start I ain't never been there so I don't know what the set-up is and for another I hear he could hold out against a whole cavalry regiment.'

'I know the set-up,' said Caleb. 'True enough, they could hold off a whole regiment, providing they were expecting them, but there are ways in and out.'

'Me an' the rest of the boys have decided that it's just about time we called off our disagreement with the folks in West Ridge,'

The Beast suddenly announced. 'We know we ain't been all that popular in town, mainly on account of the womenfolk. I guess we can understand men bein' pretty sore at us, but we're only normal men an' there ain't too many available women in town an' I guess we have taken a few liberties.'

'I'm surprised you haven't come to this decision before,' said Caleb. 'Does this mean you'll be getting together against Gill Weston?'

'Somethin' like that,' agreed The Beast.

'The point is,' said Lord Jim, 'the outlaws have never bothered us; they've left us alone and we've left them alone, but we've finally come to the conclusion that we do have some sort of social responsibility towards the town.'

The Beast and The Piper looked at Lord Jim and smiled. 'He don't always talk like that,' grinned The Piper in what Caleb took to be a broad Scots accent although he could not be certain. 'He's just puttin' on airs and graces. What he means is if we help them out they might be a little more ready to turn a blind eye to what their womenfolk get up to sometimes.'

'I think I get the picture,' grinned Caleb. 'So what are you going to do next?'

The three loggers looked at each other and shrugged. 'I guess we ain't got round to thinkin' about things like that,' said The Beast. 'All the boys are ready to act though.'

'Including Cripple Dyke?' asked Caleb.

The Beast laughed. 'I guess you could say he won't be no problem. He's just a bit more crippled than he used to be.'

Caleb had no way of knowing what had transpired at the loggers' camp and he was wise enough not to ask any questions. 'There is just one problem as I see it,' he said. 'No matter what you decide it's going to take time and if I read the situation correctly there is not too much time in the sheriff's boy's favour.'

'You mean he's on a short fuse,' said The Piper. 'OK, I suppose we'll all accept that. So, Mr Clever-Clogs Preacher, you seem to be the one with the education and, if rumour is right, you were also an officer in the army so I guess you're the natural leader. You suggest somethin'.'

Caleb was uncertain if The Piper was being sardonic or not and it was not really the time to worry about it. 'I don't think it would be a good idea to try and attack Gill Weston in his camp,' Caleb said. 'It could be that you will defeat them eventually but in the meantime it will mean the almost certain death of the sheriff's boy and probably one or two of you as well.'

'So what else do we do?' asked the sheriff.

'I see you've got your axes,' Caleb said to the three lumberjacks. The three men nodded and raised their axes slightly. 'Then I've got an idea that might just work...'

Caleb and Matt Brent peered down on to the outlaw camp from the safety of the place Caleb had used before. Their horses were tethered a few yards away but well out of sight. Below them nothing much was happening. Four of the outlaws appeared to be playing cards and the other three were just lazing about. The sheriff's boy, whose name was Aaron, appeared unharmed but was firmly tied to the same tree Caleb had tied the outlaw to. It appeared that Gill Weston was sufficiently sure of himself not to post a lookout.

'OK, that's the layout,' said Caleb. 'There's nothing much to it but you can see why it would be easy to defend. Now, getting down to Aaron is easy enough providing there's a long enough distraction for me to cut him loose.'

'You?' queried Matt Brent.

'Me!' asserted Caleb. 'You are going to provide the distraction. I mean, what could be more natural than an irate father turning up in an apparently futile attempt to save his son? If I were to suddenly show myself they'd be on their guard.'

Matt Brent sighed, smiled slightly and nodded. 'I guess you're right, yeh, it makes sense. So how do you want me to play it? I could go in guns firin' but somehow I don't think that'd do either me or Aaron any good.'

'I don't care much what you do providing you keep their attention long enough for me to get down, cut Aaron loose and get back up here.'

Matt smiled thinly. 'The way I feel right now I ain't too sure I'll be able to stop myself from shootin', still, I'll give it a try. Just promise me one thing, if it comes to a choice between savin' my boy an' leavin' me, you just make sure he gets away.'

'It's a promise,' agreed Caleb. 'Now, get back on your horse and come in along the trail as though you've just ridden from West Ridge and kick up one hell of a stink but don't go doing anything too stupid, for your boy's sake if not mine.'

'Lone rider comin' in!'

The warning call came from the one token lookout Gill Weston had posted almost at the entrance to the camp. Lone rider or not, everyone was suddenly alert, on their feet and clutching rifles.

'Who is it?' called Weston.

'Looks like that stupid sheriff,' came the response. 'Yeh, it is. What you want me to do, drop him where he is?'

'Naw,' replied Weston. 'Not unless he looks like he's goin' to start shootin'. I guess I was kinda expectin' him, it is his boy we've got. You sure he's alone?'

'Sure as anyone can be,' replied the lookout. 'There ain't no sign of anyone else.'

'He'll be alone,' said Weston. 'There ain't nobody else in West Ridge who'd have the guts to ride out here with him.'

'The Preacher?' suggested one of the men.

'He's the only one,' admitted Weston. 'OK, we don't take no chances.' He called to the lookout. 'Hold him there, tell him if he comes any closer he's a dead man.'

The message was relayed to the sheriff who obediently stopped. In the meantime Weston dispatched two men amongst the trees to search behind the sheriff. Caleb witnessed this caution and cursed silently but knew that there was nothing he could do. He had to hope that their efforts would not be directed towards him. Gill Weston made his way to where he could see and talk to the sheriff, informing him of what he was doing and why. Sheriff Brent attempted, either through good acting or a genuine desire to see his son, to shout Gill Weston down. After about ten minutes the two men returned and told their leader that they were quite certain that the sheriff was alone.

During this time Caleb had not attempted to climb down although as things turned out he would have had plenty of time. However, with all the men now gathered some thirty or so yards away from their hostage and out of his sight, he made his move. The sheriff played his part well.

'I want my boy!' he roared as he came closer. 'I ain't leavin' here without him. He ain't got nothin' at all to do with all this.'

'There's one easy way you can get him back,' grinned Weston. 'Just hand over that damned preacher.'

'How the hell can I do that?' demanded the sheriff. 'I ain't seen him since he left town.'

'Then you've got a problem,' grinned Weston.

'He could be anywhere,' insisted Brent. 'I saw a couple of the loggers an' they reckon it's more'n likely he's skipped out, headed north.'

'One of my boys says he headed that way too,' agreed Weston, 'but I got me this gut feelin' that that's just what he wants us all to think.' He laughed loudly and waved his rifle about. 'For all I know he could even be watchin' what's goin' on right now.' He turned and shouted in the general direction of where Caleb had been. 'You hear that, Mr Preacherman? I know you're out there somewhere; if you are, hear this: we've got the sheriff's boy an' Frank Hobbs is just itchin' to be let loose on him. I know you want me, so here I am, come an' get me. If you ain't showed up after Frank has finished with the boy, we'll take another an' another until you do show up.'

'And do you reckon he heard you?' scorned the sheriff.

Gill Weston shrugged and laughed. 'Who's to say? Anyhow it made me feel better if nothin' else. You get the message, Sheriff? You're likely to meet up with him 'fore anyone else, you just pass the message on.'

Caleb clamped his huge hand around Aaron Brent's mouth to prevent even the slightest sound escaping from his lips and, whilst cutting at the ropes, he gave instructions in the faintest of whispers.

'One sound out of you and we're both dead men,' Caleb whispered. 'Just do as I say, don't say nothin'. Do you understand?'

The young man attempted to nod and Caleb got the message. The last of the rope was cut away. Caleb released his hand and almost immediately had to clamp it over Aaron's mouth again as he began to demand to know what was going on. Once again Caleb repeated his order to remain silent. This time the response was more positive and Caleb led him away.

Their greatest danger was that they would be seen as they climbed the rocks. They made it without incident but almost immediately Aaron began to demand answers.

'Boy!' sighed Caleb fighting to hold his temper. 'You just come close to bein' bull-whipped to death twice now. Your pa was right, The Beast was right and Weston was right, if I had any sense at all I'd be a hundred miles away from here not caring what was happening to you. Now, do you want to stand here arguing or do you want to get the hell out of it?'

'That's my pa down there!' insisted Aaron. 'I ain't leavin' without him.'

'Do you think he doesn't know what's happening?' hissed Caleb. 'He's done his part, he's caused a diversion. Now, get on that horse, behind me and let's get going. If we hang about much longer we'll all end up dead.'

'You're in this together?' Aaron asked, incredulously.

'That's what I said,' grated Caleb. 'Now move, or do I just leave you here?'

'What about him?' persisted Aaron.

'He's a big boy, he can look after himself. Look, he's leaving!'

Matt Brent could not actually see Caleb and his son making their escape, but he judged that he had caused sufficient distraction for long enough.

'You harm one hair on that boy's body an' I'll kill you myself,' threatened the sheriff. 'I'm givin' you till dawn tomorrow to hand him back. After that I reckon the townsfolk will all be behind me. Your days are numbered, Weston.'

Gill Weston laughed and aimed his rifle at the sheriff. 'All I got to do is squeeze this trigger an' you're dead. If the folk in town see your body I don't think they'll have too much heart in comin' after me.'

'Then shoot,' invited the sheriff, turning his horse and goading it into action.

The rifle was lowered and Weston laughed again. 'Don't push your luck too far, Sheriff. Just remember what I said.'

'An' you just remember about my boy!' warned Brent as he galloped off.

'He means it too,' grunted Frank Hobbs. 'Maybe it ain't such a good idea.'

'You goin' soft?' Weston laughed. 'I

never thought I'd hear them words from you.'

'I ain't goin' soft!' scowled Hobbs. 'There just don't seem all that much point in whippin' the boy though.'

'There ain't,' agreed Weston. 'They don't know that though so as long as we've still got him we've got some control over them. Go tell the boy his old man didn't have time to stop an' talk with him.'

Frank Weston was gone no more than thirty seconds when he called out that their prisoner had gone.

'The preacher!' exclaimed Weston as he looked at the severed rope. 'There ain't nobody else it could be. Get your horses, they can't be too far away.' He raised his face to the sky, spread his arms and shouted. 'This time you've gone too far Mr Caleb Black, preacherman. This time it is you or me an' believe me, I'm goin' to make damned certain that it's you!'

TEN

Aaron Brent chose not to argue and waste any more time and Caleb pulled the young man up behind him, spurring the horse into action almost before Aaron had had time to settle. At the same time Caleb was suddenly aware of frantic activity from below. The disappearance of Aaron Brent had been discovered.

Caleb joined the main trail about fifty yards behind Matt Brent, who turned, slowed briefly but urged his horse into gallop as soon as he realized that Caleb and his son were right behind. At the same time Caleb was well aware that the outlaws were no more than fifty or sixty yards behind him and riding horses with only one man up. He dug his heels into the flanks of his horse and shouted at her to fly like the wind. Her initial reaction was to move very fast, but Caleb knew that it would not last long.

'They're gainin'!' rasped Aaron Brent. 'We don't stand no chance. Get off the trail an' among the trees, at least that way we might stand some sort of chance.'

'Just quit your jawin' boy!' ordered Caleb. 'There's a bridge just up ahead, once we're across that I don't think Weston will find it too easy.'

Aaron was tempted to ask just what the preacher was talking about but decided that he was hardly likely to get anything like a reply he would understand and clung on harder as he heard the crack of gunfire behind them. Caleb heard it too and smiled thinly, knowing that for the moment at least they were safe enough, being well out of range.

The bridge was crossed with the outlaws beginning to make headway, now no more than forty yards away. Another rifle shot reminded Caleb that they were just about within range. He attempted to urge his horse into greater speed but there was no response. In fact she seemed to be slowing up.

A fairly steep rise seemed to be just about the final effort the horse could make and by the time they reached the top, the outlaws were no more than thirty yards away and gaining rapidly. Suddenly, just as Aaron had decided that all was lost, there was a loud splintering and he looked up just in time to see a huge tree crashing earthwards across the trail almost on top of them.

However, the effect upon the pursuing outlaws was somewhat more dramatic. They had been travelling too fast to avoid the tree and all ended up tangled amongst its branches. Not only that, but another tree suddenly fell to earth not more than five or six feet further back than the first tree, effectively imprisoning the outlaws. The most distressing thing as far as Caleb was concerned were the terrified screams of the horses and he hoped that they were not injured.

'Nice timing!' grinned Caleb as he allowed his horse to slow right down to a steady walk. 'Close though, too close some might say, but it sure worked.'

'You knew about that?' asked Aaron in amazement. By that time his father had reined back and joined them.

'Sure, we knew,' said Matt. 'Caleb here had it all figured out.'

'Like I said, nice timing,' grinned Caleb, turning and waving to three figures on the edge of the trail overlooking the fallen trees.

'Yeh, nice timin',' muttered Aaron. 'Now I've seen everythin'. First of all a black preacher in West Ridge, then I owe my life to a black man, then it seems that that same black man is the only one not shit scared of Gill Weston an' then he arranges for the loggers to help. That alone is a first, them loggers ain't never helped nobody but themselves before.'

'I think you'll find things are about to change,' grinned Caleb.

'In more ways than one,' said Matt Brent. 'I didn't tell you this, mainly on account of you bein' a preacher an' such like, I didn't think you'd approve...not that I give a damn if you approve or not...but the town council has agreed to

212

a whorehouse bein' opened. The first girls should be arrivin' in about a week.'

Caleb laughed. 'Being a minister does not mean that I have no appreciation of the needs of my fellow men. Remember, I was a lieutenant in the army and that sort of background ensured that I was well educated in such matters and a whole lot more. However, were I the resident minister in West Ridge I must confess that I would be duty bound to oppose such a measure.'

'Then it's as well you ain't our regular minister,' laughed the sheriff. 'At least this way we'll get the whorehouse 'fore we gets a regular minister to spoil things.'

'And it should keep the loggers happy,' said Caleb.

The outlaws had been left to hack their own way out of the mass of tangled branches and, although Caleb's reception in town was somewhat hostile, when they heard what had happened most of them agreed that they had been a little too hard on him. Even Mrs Stein made the effort to greet him, although Caleb very quickly discovered that her prime reason was to try and enlist his support in her efforts to have the proposed whorehouse banned.

'Ma'am,' said Caleb, 'I know just how you feel and if I had any say or influence around here, I would willingly support you. As it is, I hardly think the opinion of a transient, black, preacher will have any effect at all.'

'Then the solution is simple,' declared the determined Mrs Stein. 'You must become our permanent minister. The good Lord knows that we are in desperate need of someone to lead this town out of the path of sin it has elected to follow and perhaps the fact that you are black is His way of teaching us humility and righteousness.'

Caleb had the distinct feeling that, in the opinion of Mrs Stein, having a black minister was simply a cross both she and the town of West Ridge would have to bear, at least until a more acceptable alternative came along. At that moment however, he was not prepared to argue with anyone. It had been a long and very eventful day and the prospect of a good night's sleep in a comfortable bed held out far greater attractions than debating the whys and wherefors of the proposed whorehouse.

He managed, eventually, to free himself of the verbal bonds of Mrs Stein and elected to accept the offer made by Sheriff Matt Brent to spend the night in one of the cells in the jail since there were no other residents at the time. Silas Green had made a casual suggestion that the preacher could resume residency at the hotel and, although Mrs Green had somewhat reluctantly agreed, Caleb felt that he would be safer in the jail.

Since their return to West Ridge, it appeared that hardly anyone had given any thought as to what the outlaws' next move might be although the general opinion seemed to be that Gill Weston was now a spent force in the area. This seemed to be enough for most and they appeared to assume that Weston would simply fade away. Caleb and Sheriff Brent seemed to be the only people in town who did not share this opinion.

'Twenty-four hours at the most,' declared Brent as he and Caleb indulged in a coffee and whiskey nightcap in the office. 'I can't see Weston just givin' up. Trouble is, there ain't no way of knowin' just what he'll do, but mark my words, he'll do somethin'.'

'I agree,' said Caleb, 'but I believe the idea that he is finished is correct. He'll probably make some final, defiant gesture, aimed at me if he can but against the town if he can't and that will probably be the last you'll see of him.'

'And it could be any time,' said the sheriff. 'Aaron has agreed to keep watch all night. He's a good lad, he won't fall asleep on the job. I've told him to fire two shots if he sees them.'

'Then I suppose that there is nothing else any of us can do for the moment except possibly put our faith in the Lord.'

'I'll say Amen to that,' agreed Brent. 'You had enough whiskey, Reverend?'

Caleb smiled, raised his empty glass and

peered through it at the lamp on the desk and smacked his lips. 'I do believe I could manage another. Just keep pouring, Sheriff, I'll tell you when to stop.'

A rather bleary-eyed and dishevelled Aaron Brent appeared on the steps of the office and announced that he had never spent such a long, boring and cold night before and complaining that it had all been a waste of time and that he was quite certain that Gill Weston would never dare to show his face in West Ridge again.

As the morning wore on, it did indeed appear that both Caleb and Sheriff Brent had been wrong in assuming trouble. There was even something of an air of festivity in the town. Folk seemed more relaxed and were even friendly towards the previously mistrusted black preacher. There were even a few tentative approaches from rather shy couples with requests to perform marriage and christening services, all of which he agreed to consider but did not actually commit himself to.

There was one service which he could

not refuse to perform even had he wanted to, which he did not. That morning, an elderly resident of West Ridge had been found dead in bed by his wife and, as is the way of things in the heat of the Mid-West, bodies were disposed of very quickly.

The man, Harald Svenson, originally an immigrant from Sweden, which could have been on the moon as far as most of the residents of West Ridge were concerned, had lived in the town for over forty years and it was thought, although not certain, that he was seventy five years old. That had been the age he maintained he was although his wife, also a Swede, insisted that he was over eighty.

Olga Svenson had taken the death of her husband very well, it had been expected for some weeks, but nevertheless, she seemed grateful for the few words of comfort that Caleb was able to give. The doctor declared that death was due to nothing more than old age and there was no reason not to proceed with the burial. In that respect it seemed that the undertaker,

Jake Bannon, was ahead of everyone else since he just happened to have a coffin in store the exact measurements for Harald Svenson.

The funeral was arranged for four o'clock that afternoon, partly to allow time for a grave to be dug and partly because it was far too hot before then and people would not be too pleased at having to stand around in the heat in their best and warmest clothes. Mrs Stein inevitably took charge of everything. It seemed that Mrs Stein always took charge of almost everything that happened in West Ridge which convinced Caleb that it was another good reason for not accepting the offer of becoming permanent minister in the town. This time however, he was grateful that someone had taken over arrangements leaving him free to think about his sermon and to polish up on the form of service.

Later that morning, a three-man delegation arrived from the lumberjacks' camp to make their peace with the citizens of West Ridge. The delegation consisted of the Englishman, Lord Jim as its leader, The Beast and the Irishman known as Paddy the Skunk.

In answer to Sheriff Brent's questions as to the whereabouts of Gill Weston and his men, it transpired that it had taken almost an hour for the outlaws to free themselves from the tangle of branches, but it appeared that neither they nor their horses were badly injured, nothing more than cuts and bruises. They had, of course, threatened retribution upon the loggers, but none of them believed that anything would come of it, at least not as a group. However, as a precaution, they had decided not to do any work that day and keep together. Caleb had to admit that it would take a very brave or extremely foolish man to tackle such a group of men and he believed that Gill Weston was neither brave nor foolish.

News of the proposed influx of women expressly for the purposes of pleasure, seemed to please the three and in return they promised the mayor of West Ridge, who had reluctantly agreed to meet them, that from that moment on all the married women of West Ridge would be perfectly safe and not preyed upon. Caleb did note that one of the women, when told of this decision, seemed rather disappointed.

It was Caleb who brought up the question of reward money which was due on the two men who now lay under the rubble of the fallen mine.

'By rights it belongs to The Beast, here,' said Caleb. 'I've been looking through your posters, Sheriff and it seems to me that The Beast here is entitled to four hundred dollars, three hundred for the one they called Seth and one hundred for the other one.'

'I need proof,' said the sheriff, puffing his chest out in an attempt to look officious. 'I've only got your word for it that those two are dead.'

'Are you doubting the word of a man of God?' asked Caleb, deliberately appearing to be hurt at the suggestion.

Sheriff Brent however, was unabashed. 'I trusted a preacher once, years ago, when I married my first wife, I guess you could say it taught me that even preachers are human bein's.'

'Don't tell me,' laughed Caleb, 'he ran off with your wife.'

'Ain't never seen hair nor hide of either of 'em from that day to this,' grunted Brent. 'I did hear that she'd run out him a couple of years later though an' that he'd opened up a bawdy house somewheres in California. Don't know how much truth there is in that, but it wouldn't surprise me.'

'Well this time I speak the truth,' said Caleb. 'Anyway, it's easy enough to prove, all you've got to do is dig them out. I'd take care, though, don't pull too hard on their feet, their heads are not too secure on their bodies.'

'Thanks for the warnin',' grimaced Brent. 'I can imagine what happened. I'll look into it in a day or two, I don't reckon he needs the money straight away'

The Beast agreed that he could wait and eventually the three men drifted back into the forest.

'How much are the rest of them worth?' asked Caleb.

'Why, you thinkin' of collectin'?' asked the sheriff with a slight sneer.

'Just a passing thought,' grinned Caleb. 'The Lord works in mysterious ways and it is better to be prepared.'

'Gill Weston is the big one,' said the sheriff. 'There's three thousand out on him, but then you know that. The others, not includin' the two you say are in the mine, come to...'—he wrote some figures down and then laboriously totalled them up—'eleven hundred. That's four thousand one hundred including Weston.'

'I can add up,' grinned Caleb. 'Nice money though.'

'I'd rather Gill Weston an' his men simply decided that it was time to move on,' said the sheriff. 'Bounty huntin' sure seems one hell of a hard way to earn a livin'.'

'Sometimes it's easy,' laughed Caleb, 'sometimes, like you say, it's one hell of a hard way to earn a dollar.'

Four o'clock eventually arrived and Caleb found himself cleaned up and looking more like a minister than he had for the past few days. He met the widow, Mrs Svenson in her house alone and, at her request, gave the ashen body of her late husband a private blessing, then with four stout young men acting as bearers, the coffin was taken from the front parlour of the neat little house and placed in Jake Bannon's hearse.

It seemed that the whole town had turned out for the funeral, but that was not especially because the dead man, Harald Svenson, was anyone important, it was something that always happened whenever anyone died. In a way it was nothing more than a social occasion to many, especially the women, who took the opportunity to attempt to outshine each other in their dress. Indeed, apart from Mrs Svenson and, just to be set apart from the others, Mrs Stein, nobody was dressed in black. Caleb had to admit that black suited Mrs Stein very well, making her appear a very attractive older woman which was something she seemed to realize as well.

It was Mrs Stein who, placing herself very slightly behind the preacher who was in turn escorting the widow, made the whispered observation that it did seem rather inappropriate that a minister of religion, in the process of conducting a burial service, should wear guns. Caleb pretended that he had not heard her and the procession proceeded towards the cemetery.

It was not certain who heard the shots first and it certainly did not matter. Terrified screams filled the air as folk scattered ahead of the hail of bullets which preceded seven riders racing along the street towards them. Jake Bannon's horses bolted and fled with the coffin of Harald Svenson hanging precariously, but it did not fall out, at least not within sight.

Caleb, without thinking, grabbed Mrs Svenson and Mrs Stein, pushing them behind a nearby wagon. It certainly appeared that Caleb was the main target of the outlaws and that they had seen him hide behind the wagon as the seven men began to circle the small block, firing blindly into the wagon each time they passed.

Caleb had drawn both guns and had fired several shots from one, although as far as he could see he had not hit anyone. He handed the empty gun to Mrs Stein and told her to reload it with the bullets from his gunbelts, which she did with apparently practised expertise. Suddenly Caleb realized that she too was taking aim and firing. In fact her first shot brought one of the riders from his horse and her second made certain that the writhing body was dead.

Caleb looked at Mrs Stein in a new light and she grinned back at him, almost cheekily and certainly appeared to be enjoying herself.

'I ain't had so much fun since the old wagon train days!' she exclaimed, her voice now having lost its educated refinement. 'In them days it was Injuns and even if I say so myself, I killed me my fair share of 'em.'

'I can believe it,' grinned Caleb, now

reloading his other gun. 'Keep shooting, help yourself to bullets.'

'Just try an' stop me!' laughed Mrs Stein.

After what seemed like ten or fifteen minutes but in actual fact was only three or four, other shots could be heard as Sheriff Brent and a couple of other men who had ready access to guns joined in.

Seven men had ridden into town and now five bodies lay in the street. The other two had ridden off almost as soon as the other guns had joined the fight and for a few moments nobody moved until they were certain that there was to be no further shooting.

Caleb met Sheriff Brent in the middle of the street as each examined the bodies. Three were dead and two badly injured. The sheriff called out for the doctor to see to the two injured men but looked quite disappointed.

'He got away, Gill Weston,' he sighed. 'Pity that, but I don't think we'll see him around here again.'

'Probably not,' agreed Caleb. 'The other

one was Frank Hobbs, the two most valuable of the gang.'

'Right now I ain't interested in who's worth what,' said Brent. 'Now, do you think we could get on with this funeral?'

'Just like that?' queried Caleb. 'Doesn't Mrs Svenson have a say in the matter?'

Mrs Svenson and Mrs Stein were close behind Caleb, both looking a little dishevelled and Mrs Stein especially, looking very pleased with herself. Almost reluctantly she handed Caleb his gun.

'It's been a long time since I handled one,' she smiled, 'but I haven't lost the old touch.'

'Are you all right, Mrs Svenson?' asked Caleb. 'The sheriff seems to think we ought to get on with the funeral.'

Far from being apparently distressed in any way, Mrs Svenson appeared almost happy. 'What a send off!' she laughed. 'Like Mrs Stein, Harald and I came here in the old days on a wagon train. Harald was a good shot and he too killed quite a few Indians. I think he must have really enjoyed what just happened, at least I like to think so. Sure, let's get on with it, there's no need to let a little thing like this get in the way.'

Caleb was slightly bewildered but shrugged his shoulders and dusted his clothes off. Jake Bannon's hearse, now with the coffin safely inside, returned and the procession reformed almost as if nothing had ever happened. The injured men were temporarily moved into the saloon where a young boy was given instructions to keep guard over them. The bodies of the outlaws would follow them into the cemetery later that evening, this time with no ceremony or markers on their graves.

Two days later, after performing various ceremonies, Caleb slipped quietly out of West Ridge. The only living thing to witness his departure was a small mongrel dog which gave him a cursory glance and then decided that there was something far more interesting beneath one of the boardwalks.

Caleb had not been offered nor did he claim any part of the few hundred dollars reward on the dead and injured men. Sheriff Brent had stated, quite logically, that it was impossible to say who had shot whom and therefore the reward should go to the town funds.

When he had first ridden into West Ridge, Caleb's general direction had been north, not that he had anywhere particular in mind to go, but there seemed no reason why he should change his mind now. He had been assured that the trail eventually came out on to more open country after passing through the forest and close to the camp where the outlaws had been.

He felt almost at home as he slowly made his way through the forest, but he knew he would not be sorry when it was behind him, he was not really at home amongst trees, he was more of an open country man.

He supposed that he must have travelled about ten miles; certainly he had passed the outlaw camp and found it quite easy to resist the temptation to take another look. The river had been forded easily three or four miles back, when he had the feeling that he was being observed. There was nothing to see, no sounds, just a feeling.

The feeling persisted even though he had made several attempts at climbing to high points to see if anyone was following. Eventually he decided that it was nothing more than imagination or possibly the animals of the forest. He could not be certain, but he was quite convinced that he had seen a bear nearby, but it did not seem to take any interest in him.

Suddenly his previous feelings of being watched were amplified in startling reality as a shot echoed through the trees, his hat flew into the air and a searing pain pierced his head. For a few moments everything blacked and when he came to he was lying on the ground.

He was quite alert, obviously not badly injured, but the instinct to survive made him remain where he was, perfectly still. Nothing seemed to happen for quite a few minutes and something crawling up his face and into his nostril almost forced Caleb to move. A very quick but hard blow down the nostril seemed to clear the offending insect.

A faint movement behind him told Caleb that someone or something was coming towards him. The scuff of a boot on stone confirmed that it was human and not animal.

'Dead?' asked a voice.

'Looks like it,' said another voice which Caleb instantly recognized as being Gill Weston. 'Pity if he is, I'd've enjoyed seein' his hide bein' stripped off a piece at a time'

'I was beginnin' to think he'd either stayed in West Ridge or gone another way,' said Frank Hobbs. 'What we goin' to do now?'

'Move on, I guess,' replied Weston. 'It's all finished at West Ridge now them loggers have taken sides with the townsfolk.'

'Him?' queried Hobbs.

'Wolf meat,' laughed Weston. 'Strip what you want off him and his horse. The horse can look after itself.'

Gill Weston strode past Caleb, intent on recovering whatever he could from the saddle-bags and Frank Hobbs roughly turned over what he thought was a dead body. He never did turn Caleb over completely...

The first shot, into Frank Hobb's face, was so close that Caleb was momentarily blinded by spraying blood and bone. The second shot slammed into Gill Weston's body as he turned, almost in slow motion and for a few moments Caleb remained where he was, with the body of Frank Hobbs pinning him down, waiting for any movement from Gill Weston. There was none and slowly Caleb stood up, feeling distinctly groggy.

Gill Weston proved to be alive, but only just. Defiantly, Weston spat weakly at Caleb as the black preacher towered above him, gun ready to deliver the final shot should it be necessary.

'You sure you're a preacher an' not the Devil?' croaked Weston. 'I hear cats have nine lives, I reckon you've got a never endin' supply'

'I bleed just like any other man,' replied

Caleb, pointing to the blood oozing down his cheek. 'It's even the same colour as yours. Maybe you need a bit more practice at shooting. I don't know if you'll get any practice in where you're going, but wherever it is, you won't be able to kill anyone else, they'll be dead already. Perhaps we'll meet there again one day.'

'I'll arrange a reception,' hissed Weston, attempting to spit again but failing. He gasped, stared wide eyed at Caleb for a moment and then coughed. 'Damn your black hide, Mr Preacherman...'

'I was kinda hopin' we'd seen the last of you,' sighed Sheriff Matt Brent as Caleb reined in his horse outside the office. 'Now don't tell, let me guess who you've got there...' He nodded at the two horses Caleb had in tow with two bodies slung across each saddle. 'Three thousand four hundred dollars of outlaw. Nice payday.'

'There are easier ways of earning a living,' smiled Caleb, 'but I'm not complaining.'

'And what will you do with that much

money?' asked Brent. 'Just bein' a preacher don't mean that some punk won't shoot you for that much.'

'I have plans for it,' smiled Caleb.

Once again, at the first hint of dawn, Caleb Black, preacher, slipped out of West Ridge, this time a much richer man. Unlike the first time when he headed north, this time Caleb headed south, the direction from which he had entered town. On this occasion he had a very definite destination in mind, the remote home of the couple who had given him food and shelter before he reached West Ridge. As was fairly normal for him, Caleb decided that there were far more deserving causes and some people with a far greater need of so much money than he had...

This Large Print Book for the Partially sighted, who cannot read normal print, is published under the auspices of

THE ULVERSCROFT FOUNDATION

THE ULVERSCROFT FOUNDATION

. . . we hope that you have enjoyed this Large Print Book. Please think for a moment about those people who have worse eyesight problems than you . . . and are unable to even read or enjoy Large Print, without great difficulty.

You can help them by sending a donation, large or small to:

**The Ulverscroft Foundation,
1, The Green, Bradgate Road,
Anstey, Leicestershire, LE7 7FU,
England.**

or request a copy of our brochure for more details.

The Foundation will use all your help to assist those people who are handicapped by various sight problems and need special attention.

Thank you very much for your help.